Crossed Genres

Year One

Crossed Genres

Year One

EDITED BY BART R. LEIB AND K.T. HOLT

CROSSED GENRES: YEAR ONE

http://crossedgenres.com

———————————

TABLE OF CONTENTS

The Time of Tales

C.L. Rossman

The loud *boing, boing, boing* jarred her straight out of sleep and into an unwelcome world. One eyelid peeled back to reveal a rather annoyed gray-blue eye. The comset was chiming, not just accepting a message. She must have left the aural function on.

"*Vrakking* machine," she mumbled from under a pile of furs, "I thought I shut you off last night."

The vrakking machine didn't answer. It just went on pounding out the chimes in pulses of three.

"Frost it," she said and pushed her way out of her warm bed. She'd have to answer. Unwise decision to keep a comset in her bed chamber.

"The Time of Tales, An-katrae speaking," she answered.

"Day's light, *chai-tautsche*!" came the voice at the other end, with unwarranted cheer. "This is Huralen at the trophy hall tower. Are you ready for some company, An-katrae?"

"*H'vack!* Where?" she gasped, clutching her disheveled mane. "Travelers, Huralen? Where are they? When are they coming?" *I have to get the lodge ready, start a fire, start the stewpot—*

"Not on the nock, auntie. Perhaps this afternoon or evening." The comset operator sounded taken aback. "Is this a bad time?"

"T'chak," she lied, not successfully. "I—have to prepare, that's all. Can you tell me how many, *chai-tautsche*?"

"Churr; just one. A trade ship stopped here late last night and their hired hunter immediately got off and wanted to know where he could stay *in private* during the planetide. The Prime Hunt couple gave him your coordinates, and he said chak, he'd be there after he hunted today."

"Krr…" She had a few tare' in which to clean up, then. "Good. I can handle that. What's his name, Huralen?"

He hesitated, then said, "I…krr…don't know, An-katrae. Our Prime Hunters just passed the message on to me this morning. They didn't mention a

1

name."

"Never trouble, no doubt he'll tell me himself. My thanks, Huralen. And tell the Prime Hunt couple I'm honored that they thought of me. Signing out," and she disconnected before he could say any more.

She turned off the chimes, leaving the message reminder on blinking light only. She dressed heedlessly, left her room and headed for the steps in the hall. If someone was coming, she'd better get busy.

And a hunter, too, the operator said. True, all her people were called *tautschen* or Hunters, but not all of them hunted for a living. Like herself. She was a fairly good shot and had gone through training in her youth, but never had a Master Hunt.

No, her passion lay in other things: in reading and in the activity which gave her the name Storyteller. It was part of the reason she ran this little lodge in the woods.

The lodge had two levels: a big hearth with deep comfortable chairs, a buffet table and a cookroom on the first floor; six bedchambers plus hers on the second. Her joy in life was to host people and listen to their stories. She'd save the best tales, asking permission to write them down and publish them on one of her online story sheets or in a book. That, more than her little lodge, made her a living.

She thought about all this as she dashed downstairs, trying not trip on her own toeclaws. She hadn't had visitors in nearly two tendays, and she'd let the place go lax.

She took the staircase's last 90-degree turn and halted four steps above the floor, staring. The lodge was clean. The massive wood buffet table gleamed golden, polished and dust-free. To the far right, flames danced in the stone hearth. And from behind the door to the cookroom, she swore she could hear the rattle of a lid on a pot of stew, bubbling.

"Why, those little dear ones," she murmured. "They must have come in and done this." She'd hired two of the freehold's youngsters, a boy and a girl, to assist her when she had guests. "Someone must have told them to come today.

"I owe them my thanks, later," she promised as she looked down at her hands. Her long-taloned fingers moved, half-clenched, uncurled. Not bad today. Sometimes the bone-biter disease was worse, paining her so she could barely move her fingers—and she could not do all that she needed and loved to do. She couldn't even write those stories down.

She took anti-inflammatories to ease her pain, but the healers wanted her to have surgery, so they could shave down the awkward bony spurs.

She wasn't ready for that yet. Maybe sometime. If the pain became unbearable. Later. Not right now.

*

"Aroh, the lodge!" she heard from outside later that afternoon. She hurried to the front door and looked out.

And there he was, a strapping broad-shouldered Hunter in full field gear, standing on a slight rise clear of the trees.

An-katrae pushed the door open and called, "Day's-light, vr'hunter! It's a public house; come straight in!"

He smiled, tilted his head back, and returned, "It does no harm to call out first, either!" Then he came up the path in confident and powerful strides.

She retreated a polite distance from the door and he came in, saying, "I was told to seek 'the Storyteller's house' at these coordinates, honored lady, so I had to make sure."

She smiled. "Well, you've found it. The Storyteller would be me, An-katrae, and this is my lodge, The Time of Tales, where I'm honored to put up guests. And you, vr'hunter?"

"Oh, chak—let me put this down and greet you properly"—and he swung a small skinny *teveh* off his shoulder, set it carefully on the floor, swiped his hands on his thigh guards and then extended them, turning the wrists outwards and saying, "I am Draemar, a master hunter from Six Systems, and I am honored, An-katrae."

He had a carefully firm grip, a pleasant smile, and didn't seem like someone who wanted to be left alone. She decided not to mention that, at least for now.

After the greeting, he told her, "I'm off the trade ship Charevan's Heart, which made planetide at the freehold port; and I need someplace to den up for about four nights. May I stay here, milady?"

He was the *ship's* hunter, then, not a trophy hunter, and he had good manners, so she agreed.

"On-course you may stay, vr'hunter. You have your choice of rooms this season; and my fee..."

"Churr?"

"My fee is light: a small pelt or cut of meat per night, or a larger for the whole span."

"Ah." He glanced down at the teveh, hoisted it. "Then this may start it."

"...and a story," she finished, watching him.

Startled, his glance flew back to her. "A—what, milady?"

She clasped her hands below her waist; they had begun to hurt. "A story. Yours, or one you know. Just one. I collect them, you see."

"Stories?" He looked as if he didn't believe what he was hearing. Doubt shaded his face.

"Yes, it's my...avocation. How I got my name. Look here, vr'hunter, if you will;" and she led him closer to the hearth. She pointed to a wall shelf to one side of and above the hearth. Small bound books half-filled it. "Those are the results of years of travelers' tales, told to me one at a time. After I get enough of them for a little book, I bind them or record them into computer flat-circles. I used to write them down by hand, but you see..." she held up her hands and laughed as if to pass them off.

"I…see," he said gravely. "A hard trail for a writer. But An-katrae, what if I *don't* have a story? Will you throw me out?" Half-joking but half-serious too, his head cocked to one side.

She flapped her hands. "Oh, t'chak! Spirit, no! I never turn aside a guest"—*and he was the first one in a long time*—"Here, think nothing of it, Esteemed Hunter, but go and take your rest in your choice of room. They're on the second level."

He held up the teveh.

"There's a skinning-shed behind the lodge, and freezers inside, behind the cookroom," she said. "And a nice bathing alcove toward the back—you'll pass it going out. Are you hungry? I can have citrus, broth and stew for you at once or later. No one will disturb you here, not even me."

He stood listening to this waterfall of words and when it finally abated, said very gently, "Honored, mistress. About a *tare'* later for main-meat, if you would. And please call me Draemar. Your pardon; I'll go prepare this;" and he took off, graciously but with expedience, for the skinning-shed

And there went her chance for a story, *d'faal.*

*

She didn't think she'd see him again until main-meat, but he popped back in 15 *kt'tare* later, holding a bloody tube-shaped cut of meat and said, "A backstrap from the teveh, milady; you and I can both enjoy it tonight. And I'll start the pelt drying, too."

Then he left again before she could thank him.

She put bowls and trenchers on the common table, turned the heat down under the massive cook pot to "simmer," then set up an automatic turnspit over the hearthfire so she could roast the tenderloin there, and spitted it on. She could have cooked it in the oven, but fire-seared meat tasted so much better! She set a few more logs on the fire and sat down in one of the hearthside chairs to rub her aching wrists.

Perhaps she shouldn't have mentioned the story; it almost put him to flight. It *was* a disappointment, but she'd rather have the guest. And if the hunter wanted quiet and solitude, why then, he deserved to have them.

She sighed and leaned back in the chair, grateful to rest.

She heard water running in the baths a short time later, and a luxurious splashing. He enjoyed a hot bath when he got one, it seemed.

Sometime later, he came back into the hearthroom, his long auburn mane wet and tied back, the moisture fairly steaming from his body. He had a drying pelt round his shoulders and a loincloth round his hips; but he'd stripped off most of his gear to wash and stow away, she guessed, and he was quite a handsome hunter. Of a bronzy-gold base color with warm brown eyes and perfect black rosettes mottling his back and flanks, he was too broad-shouldered to be pure

Plains Clan, though he had their markings. A hybrid, then, like most freeholders.

"Greetings, milady," he hailed her, smiling and happy. "Your baths are wonderful. They've revived me already."

She returned the smile. "Are you ready for main-meat?" She started to rise.

"Oh, chak! But hold, hold; I'll get it. I'll bring it to the hearth." And he whisked the pelt off his shoulders to hang over a chair while he went to fetch the food.

"Really, Draemar, you're a guest. I should"—

"Sit where you are and take your ease," he laughed. "I'm hale and I know my way around a cookroom. Sit there, please."

And he was as good as his word. He cut up meat into the stew and set other parts of it, like ribs and roasts, into the oven to bake. Then he brought his prize, another roll of muscle-meat half-a-kri long, to set on the fire besides the first.

"*Two* tenderloins?" she asked. "You're not giving me both of those, are you? Because I asked for just one piece…"

Another laugh. "Trante, trante, good storyteller. This is just a small teveh. I figure you and I can dispose of it during my time here, especially since I don't have a story to pay you with!"

"Krr, but…"

"T'chak, no *doubts* either," he teased, his eyes sparkling; and she could imagine how he must fascinate and frustrate unbonded huntresses. A strong handsome hunter with a sense of humor: the ladies must be ready to claw each other to get his attention…

He wouldn't bother *her*, she decided. "On-stat, then. Do your worst."

That only made him laugh; and he served main-meat as gracefully as a clan chef to his chieftain.

They ate a tenderloin first, pronouncing it delicious, and afterward sat in front of the crackling fire, savoring cups of citrus and listening to the trees shiver in the wind outside.

Draemar became quieter after eating, unlike most *tautschen*, who feed silently and become social afterward. It was that time, the Time of Tales, which gave her guest-house its name.

But if he wanted to be silent, it didn't trouble *her*. An-katrae pulled out her recorder and inserted a small data crystal. She pulled her style-board off a shelf, stuffed the interior with paper, then sat down again opposite him.

He glanced up, smiled, and returned to contemplating the fire.

An-katrae put on the earphones, keyed in the print function on the style board, opened the keypad, and prepared to type another story. She still had a few she hadn't printed out yet, and since her wrists were not too painful, she might be able to do part of one now.

If only it didn't rain…

She switched the recorder on low and began to transcribe.

She sensed the hunter's immediate interest. The audio should be on too low to disturb him, so this must be normal *tautschen* curiosity surfacing.

He didn't ask her a question at once, which surprised her. But when she tried to ignore that light sense of interest across from her, she found she could not. She struggled to transcribe, managed to tap out an entire page, but the weight of being watched grew heavier and heavier until she couldn't stand it anymore. She pulled the earphones off and raised her head.

He wasn't even looking at her. But he did look then, a question in his eyes.

"I wouldn't have disturbed you, milady."

"T'churr, never mind. Some of my stories are nested in here," she told him, lifting the instrument.

Encouraged, he asked, "And you're putting them in a file—or on paper?"

"Both, really. When I get enough in *here*"—tapping the style board box with a fore-talon—"then I can bind them into one of those;" and she pointed to the bookshelves over his head.

He craned to see. "Your little books?"

"Churr," she beamed, "filled with stories of adventures from hunters, traders, explorers. Every one different, every one true."

Draemar gave a long appreciative "Churr...urr...I see. And that is why your lodge bears its name."

"Chak." She settled back, satisfied. "It hears plenty of tales. And I can print as many copies of a booklet as I like—I sell them, too, and give them to some children and families here."

The hunter got up from his chair and ranged back and forth below the bookshelves." Krr...Travelers' Tales 1; Hearthside Tales; Hunters' Stories 4—each not very big but each with its own name." He started to reach out towards one but stopped and glanced back at her, uncertain.

She made a nudging motion with her chin. "Go on, vr'hunter; they are here for my guests to read as well."

"Ah, I am honored, milady," he said with that wonderful Hunt courtesy, and plucked one of the thin little books off the shelf—a "Hunters' Tales," naturally.

He settled back in his chair, lifted his glass of citrus again and began delicately turning the pages with his thumbclaw. Apparently he found something interesting there, for he gave a little "*hunh*" underbreath and did not speak again.

An-katrae went back to her transcribing.

*

The fire gave a startling *pop* and she jerked awake. *Asleep, old tautsche?* She scolded herself. *What will the hunter think?*

The fire-snap seemed to have startled her guest, too, for he looked up, glanced from the fire to her, and said, "I didn't realize the *tare'* was so late. I should go to bed; I have to hunt in the morning."

"Again?"

A slight smile. "For the trade ship this time. Something bigger than a little teveh. They have seven *tautschen* aboard ship, all family and all hungry... Your lodge is a pleasant relief from the crowd, storyteller."

"Churr, churr, honored." She eased herself to her feet. "I should get some sleep, too, but first I need to clean this place up."

And was surprised again when he almost leaped from his chair and got in front of her, saying, "Let me do that, An-katrae. There are just a few things to wash, and I can bank this fire and have it ready for morning—doing it even as he spoke. "There is nothing so delectable as a backstrap braised on the fire, t'churr?"

"But I"—she tried to protest, but the hunter was speed itself, doing most of the simple chores in the time it took her to get to the buffet table across the room.

"There. Done," he said, grinning saucily at her. "No trouble, milady."

She had to smile. "I should have you around here to do all the cooking and cleanup, vr'hunter; youth is so expedient."

He laughed. "Just more impatient, I think. I *was* going to ask a favor, though..."

"H'vack?"

He held up the thin little book. "I'm almost finished with this, and if I might borrow it...?"

"Chak. As long as you are in my lodge, Draemar, you may read any of these. Take them to your room if you like. I find that reading helps me sleep."

"Me, too," he confessed, "though some hunting tales keep me awake. Well and good, milady. Thank you and night's-rest to you."

"Night's-rest to you, too, Draemar."

And then he was gone, leaving her with nothing to do except set her wake-time in the morning. If he went hunting, he'd need provisions; and she didn't want to miss him going out.

*

She did, though. She rose early to confront an empty lodge and a day of gray autumnal rain. Her wrists were already afire.

Cold and wet, may you have good hunting indeed, Draemar—and watch your footing, she thought as she wrapped both wrists in white gauze in order to carry on.

She cleaned the hearth and added water to the stewpots; then, since she couldn't do any more transcribing, she might as well use the opportunity to just sit and read.

She decided to light a fire after all—not that she needed it to support the inset geothermal system, but it *did* make an ancient statement of comfort against the cold, light against the dark.

Done, she sat down beside it with a book in her hands. But she didn't read it. Instead, she sat staring into the flames, and wondered how the hunter was faring.

*

He returned early, just after high sun, or what would have been high sun had it not been raining. This time he dragged an air-sled behind him.

"All I caught were two large birds and a small—something—that eats plants," he grumbled as he lifted them off. "Nowhere near enough to feed a trade ship. Here, you may as well have them, milady storyteller."

He almost handed them to her before he noticed her bound wrists and corrected: "T'churr, never trouble. I'll just put them up in your freezer," and he made for the back rooms, towing the sled behind him.

An-katrae hurried after him. "Vr'hunter! Draemar," she called just as he pushed open the back door.

"Churr?"

"Do you need larger animals to hunt? Because I know where you can find some."

That stopped him. "You do?"

He drew up, all attention, and she fumbled a bit, telling him:

"We have a larger beast, about krolf-size, that browses on the river plains just southeast of here. The Beast with Two Heads, we call it."

He leaned forward. "It has two heads? I'd like to see that! And how far southeast is this river? Can you show me?"

She could, on a computer map, and he came back to the hearthroom to see.

"*Krr*...that's not two kri-veh from here! And what time of day are they abroad, An-katrae, do you know?"

"On-path I do! I'm—I used to be a good shot, myself, before...*t'chrrt*! Look for them at twilight and dawn. Or earlier, in dim weather like this."

That perked him up. "Aroh, storyteller! That's a fine tale to a hunter's ears. Now let me clean this catch and dry myself off. I can start hunting again in two *tare'*. And thank *you*, An-katrae, I am honored."

He raced through skinning and butchering the small game, stuck a fine plump ground-fowl on the turnspit for tonight. Then he bathed just as quickly and returned to rest before the fire, eating a slice of roasted tenderloin and drinking a cup of hot broth before he had to go out again.

An-katrae tried to work some more on her recording, but her wrists pained her so much she set it aside and kept the hunter company at the fire, a cup of broth in her hand.

He had leaned back and closed his eyes to relax a bit before going out again. That didn't dull his observational powers, however, for he opened one eye a slit and remarked,

"Mmm-rrr...they have auto-speech boards now, milady. You speak or play a recording into it and it comes out in print."

She glanced at him, looked away. "I know."

"Your pardon," the hunter mumbled and started to withdraw. "I thank you for the game beasts' information."

"No offense. Really, Draemar. Sit and enjoy your drink. It will be a bitter night."

He sat, but not for long. After another half-tare he excused himself and went to prepare for an early hunt.

An-katrae thought she must have been too abrupt with him. Just because she couldn't afford the new machine didn't make it *his* fault, *d'faal.* She puttered around the hearthroom until he came out of his room again and she gave him a heartfelt, "Good hunting!"

He grinned and gave back a cheerful, "Let fall Chance!" before he went out the door.

"Oh, I hope not," she murmured as she watched him jog off into the mist and rain.

*

He didn't come back that night. Nor before dawn. An-katrae spent a sleepless evening waiting for him.

But then just after sunrise, she heard a hearty "Aroh, the lodge!" outside and she rushed to the door.

"Draemar!" she cried, "You've come back"—sounding like some love-struck cub, she realized too late.

He didn't seem to notice. "Chak!" he shouted, and gestured at the sled behind him. A huge lumpy shape lay on it, limbs asprawl. "And you did give me good hunting, An-katrae: I took three of these beasts. I had to stop at the trophy hall before I came here, to give the traders their share—the other two."

"But this one...?" she began, craning to see it.

"...is for you. The meat and hide. Though I'll keep the head, milady, for hunter's share." He flashed her that insouciant smile and tugged the sled forward.

She came out to stand on the deck. "But Draemar, that's far too much. You've already given me several animals, more than enough—"

"Tsck," he clicked at her, turning to steer round the lodge so he could get at the skinning shed in back. "I had no story, remember?"

"Churr; but all this..."

"Is fair hideshare, Storyteller. It will last through many guests."

And she guessed he thought she was rather poor, and he could help, though he'd never say so outright.

I am not poor, she thought, then flinched when pain flashed through her wrists. *But I do need help*, she admitted, which put her hackles down.

"I'll open the shed for you, Draemar; it's locked," she said, quite mild now.

As she hurried back through the lodge to meet him at the door, she realized she was still holding something—her recorder and styleboard. To late to re-shelve them now. She jammed the recorder into her furry sweater pocket and the styleboard under her belt, and went on to the shed.

He went in, sled and all, as soon as she opened the door. "Prrt! Thank you, milady; I'll have this skinned and quartered in a short-throw and ...*krr*...I can see why you call it a two-headed beast." He lined the sled up with a cutting table and heaved the beast onto it.

She smiled. "Can you now? Did it give you any trouble?'

"T'chak, not once I got near enough to see that this big knob on the end"— he pulled up the large, shaggy head-shaped bump at the end of the spine—"is really a tail; though the creature carries it upright as if it *were* a head. I can see why predators would be uncertain about which end to attack, t'churr?"

"Churr," she agreed, laughing. "But you figured it out, vr'hunter. You would have even if I hadn't told you its name."

"Perhaps," he said, smiling. He rolled the big creature onto its back, prepared to begin skinning at the long visceral slit. "It gave me an interesting hunt, even so."

She leaned in, curious, so he told her about it: how he first came upon the creatures' great wet footprints in the lowlands, then saw the beasts themselves through the screen of trees, and how he crept close, stalking them.

It was a good story, and if he didn't mind telling it, she didn't mind listening. Apparently Draemar was a sociable fellow, taken one-on-one. She wondered why he'd taken a contract on such a crowded trade ship to begin with...

But she couldn't politely ask, though she *could* politely excuse herself once he ran out of words, saying, "I need to put that bird on to reheat, Draemar, so main-meat will be ready when you are. Thank you for telling me about your hunt; it makes a good story."

"*Unh,*" he grunted in surprise, "so that's was what you meant by 'giving you a story?' Just that little bit?'

"It's all most hunters or traders talk about, bits and pieces of their lives, usually, which I weave into little tales. You see, it's not difficult at all." And she left *him* with the "interested look" this time.

"That's probably all the story I'll get from him, too," she said as she set the bird to warm. "And not for publication. Yet here I am still carrying this"—she reached down to pull styleboard and recorder from her clothing.

When she saw the little blue light on the recorder, bright and unblinking, she nearly dropped the device. It was *on;* somehow it had turned on by accident when she jammed it in her pocket. She stared at it for several moments, then carefully switched it off.

She couldn't help but smile.

Willing or not, the hunter had given her a story after all.

*

After finishing up, the hunter went directly to bed, saying he would be down for main-meat after a few *tare's* rest.

"No trouble," An-katrae told him. The big bird would take a while to heat up thoroughly, and she could add juices to tenderize it while she waited. She didn't have a chance to tell Draemar she'd recorded him by mistake.

Maybe later.

*

The heavy *thump-thump* of fire-logs rolling into the bin outside woke her from a half-drowse. She threw on a fur and hurried out to see Gharaith, the "helper" children's father, cheerfully rolling a supply of firewood into the covered bin.

"Ghariath," she greeted the hunter, "thank you for bringing the wood."

"My honor, An-katrae," he returned. "Do you want me to carry some in for you?"

"Just a few armloads, if you would. Your children usually do that for me."

"Chak, I remember," he said. He loaded up and brought her a big armful. "How is everything with you, honored one? Are your thermal units working? Do you need any repairs?"

"T'churr, not at the moment. Everything's fine, by good Chance." Here was another hunter looking after her—why had she never noticed it till now? "Will you stop for a cup of broth or citrus, vr' hunter?"

He looked regretful. "I'm honored, but I cannot. Aleyn and the little ones are waiting for me to come back so we can go to the trade fair. Would you like to go with us, An-katrae?"

"Oh, no—I'm honored, but I have to stay here and care for my guest, the trade ship hunter."

"Krr-rr…it's good to be busy, anypath. Will you want our two young *kaels* to come for a few more mornings then?"

"Yes, for two, I think. And tell them I have new books waiting for them. And…vr'hunter, hold a moment, please." She left him wondering while she went back inside the lodge to bring him payment for the wood—a shoulder roast from the new beast.

She insisted he take it, despite his protestations, and he finally did, saying, "You pay too much, milady. You must treat your guests like clan leaders in your lodge!"

She laughed and shooed him back to his family.

When she came back inside, she saw Draemar standing on the stairs, evidently wakened by the noise.

"I'll make up for it tonight," he assured her when she tried to apologize. "A good long sleep, dark to dawn, for a change. Now, how is that bird doing?"

*

They spent this afternoon as they had the first one, eating in silence, then sitting by the fire. There, An-katrae felt she had to tell him she had recorded his

11

words by accident.

"I crave your pardon, Draemar," she said. "I'll delete them if you like."

"But you haven't yet, *t'churr*?" he said, sounding amused.

"No, I"—Flustered, she found herself blushing. She reached for the recorder.

The hunter stopped her with a gentle touch. "Hold, please. Let me hear it, first."

She replayed it and he listened, cocking his head like an attentive bird.

And when she came to the end...

"...that is the first time I've ever *heard* myself," he remarked. "On-stat, milady, keep the recording if you like, even though it's a rather dull hunting tale."

"I'm honored. You've had harder hunts?"

"Many times. Why, the worst hunt I've ever had was..." He saw her finger twitch, and he smiled. "Yes, you may record this too, Storyteller, if I can kept a clawhold on my nerves."

And after a few moments his delivery smoothed over and he told his story, his eyes drifting back into memory.

An-katrae got it all. After he finished she couldn't help telling him: "That's a chilling story! If I use them both, I'll have enough for another little book."

"It will be in a book? Like one of these? I'm flattered, milady."

"I'll send you a copy if you like. Over the comset. Where does your trade ship make tie next, Draemar?"

"Krr, at Cloud Systems Station, where I'll meet my wife."

"Your *wife*!" she exploded

He blinked. "Churr. Why are you so surprised? Didn't you think I would be bonded? Though I didn't tell you; my error, An-katrae."

She sighed. "Oh, it's not that, Esteemed Hunter. With the effect you must have on huntresses, I thought it would be difficult for you to choose one."

And knew at once she'd gone too far.

His eyes widened and his jaw dropped, showing his lower biting teeth.

"The *effect* I must have...hard to *choose?*" he repeated.

"Ahai, vr'hunter, forgive me!" she cried out, almost reached to touch his arm. She checked her movement, started to withdraw. "I shouldn't have..."

He caught her errant hand—gently, by the wrist, and held it, looking as if two emotions fought in him. He struggled for words.

"On that 'cast...on that 'cast..." He tried, nearly choked, tried again: "You say true, Lady Storyteller—and it *still* surprises me. I did have a great share of attention when I was younger. As a 23-year-old just starting out, not even mature, I found it almost overwhelming."

He looked directly into her eyes and said, "But. I have to say...I like to hear it *still.*" And he smiled and let her go.

She was so upset she didn't know what to say. A *tautsche* of her age! He'd think she wanted...wanted...

Then she caught his eyes, noticed the wicked glint in them, and before she could puff up in protest, he grinned, winked at her and said, "And a comely *tautsche's* interest is always appreciated, even now." He chuckled.

She gasped, pulled back, tried to scold him, but words wouldn't come— "You—you *kael,* you!" she cried, which made him laugh out loud—and so did she, a moment later.

They ended the evening with the comfortable conversation of old friends.

*

The trade fair lasted only two more days—two blustery, wind-chilled days, with rain slashing through now and then.

Draemar spent most of those two days at the lodge, resting and reading, but also helping out where he could. He finished curing the big animal's hide for her, and did a few minor repairs to the stairs inside the lodge.

"I'm not much of a woodworker," he said, "but I think these will hold together."

And later, he practiced his *tch-won'*—those fighting skills she'd heard so much about. He chose an old tree stump out back as his 'opponent,' and An-katrae peeped from the windows to see him make flying leaps, spins and difficult combat maneuvers, which were wonderful to behold.

On the second day, he went to see the traders, taking his sled with him.

"Would you like anything from the trade ship, An-katrae?" he asked. "It has tools and home goods and appliances, as well as weapons."

"Oh, t'churr; I'm on-stat. I have everything I need," she tried to assure him, and could tell he didn't believe a word of it.

But the only comment he made was a thoughtful "Krr..." as he left, and promised to be back within a few *tare'*.

*

He was, well before sunset, and his once-empty sled carried a large, hide-wrapped lump.

"A good trading day, Storyteller!" he roared cheerfully at her. So it seems they were back on their old friendly footing. Draemar took his "package" upstairs with him, leaving the sled tied outside, and An-katrae wondered why he hadn't just left his goods aboard ship.

He was in high good humor when he came down, though, as close to excited as she'd ever seen him.

"Zarahane is already at the space station," he told her; "and after we breaktie at sunrise tomorrow, I'll be with her in less than two days!"

"Well and good, Draemar. Is Zarahane your wife?"

"Oh, churr. Your pardon, An-katrae, I didn't give you her name. But yes, and after I arrive and claim hunter's share of the ship's goods, she and I are going to pick a planet here in Cloud Systems to settle on."

13

She tried to be light-hearted for him, but her words felt heavy. "No more star-roving for you then, vr'hunter?"

"Krr, not for a while, anypath. Not until after we have children and see them grown." His keen eyes detected her mood and he said softly, "I have had a good stay here, honored one, quiet and in good company, and I appreciate it."

Then more gently still: "An-katrae, if you need anything of me, I would give it to you, you know. Only ask. It would be my honor." He looked at her, into her, and she knew he meant it, as a hunter oath-bound. He would even have given her the *ashe-kvar* in that moment, she believed.

She corralled her wild desires. She would not trouble him or the huntress he loved. Instead, she forced herself to meet his eyes and say, "Nothing, Draemar, except perhaps you could send to me from your chosen planet, and let me know you've come safe home."

He gave her a long warm look and a smile, very unlike his usual boisterous grin, and said, "Hunt and done, milady, I shall take your comset address and send to you before AND after." And he hooked a forefinger talon gently under one of hers, and lifting her hand, raised it to touch his chest above the heart, once, then set it back down. He inclined his head, thrilling her—and went on to help her with main-meat and to act completely normal again.

Lounging before the fire, they had their last evening together.

*

As usual she did not wake early enough to see him go. She *meant* to; she dragged herself out from under warm furs two *tare'* before sunrise. But when she came downstairs looking for him, the lodge was empty and silent. She felt a swift, solid pain to the heart, and tried to tell herself that he had been only a guest, after all.

Then she noticed *the object* sitting on her buffet table and approached it with caution. When she saw what it was, she gasped, and knew why Draemar had gone along to the trade fair that day, and why he'd brought his purchase back to her lodge...

...so he could leave it here.

He'd bought her a fully-automated recorder-transcriber and the styleboard with it—one that you had only to speak into or play a recording and the words would appear as text and print. You could print it out from there.

A note scribbled on a hidescrap lay on top if it. She reached out with a trembling hand.

It said: "Now you can make as many little books as you like, An-katrae, and tell your own story, too. I would like to read it, myself—Draemar."

"Oh you frosted foolish *wonderful* hunter!" she breathed, running her fingers over the device. "How can I ever repay you for this? You should have bought something for *yourself* instead."

Evidently, he knew her very thoughts, for when she turned the hidescrap over, she saw another post on the other side. And it read: "You *must* use this, Storyteller. It is a regard-gift and you are honor-bound to accept!"

"Honor-bound!" She exclaimed and laughed, then started to cry. She sank down into a nearby chair with the wonderful machine clutched to her.

"Oh, Draemar, may you have safe harbor indeed," she whispered, and sighed.

She didn't know how long she sat there; it was quiet and pleasant and her thoughts ran far away.

But a familiar sound brought them back. A persistent three-tone chime broke through her mental cloud at last, and she recognized it…

"The comset," she said, sitting up. Could it be Draemar, calling back so soon? Carefully she put the transcriber back down on the table and went to answer the com.

"The Time of Tales, An-katrae speaking," her voice quavered.

"Is that you, honored storyteller? I hardly recognize you," said a familiar voice, though not the one she'd hoped for… "Your pardon, this is Huralen. I'm on com duty again, and the Prime Hunt Couple asked me to call you."

"They did?" She controlled her disappointment and tried to speak normally. "Krr…I mean yes, Huralen, it's me."

Relief at the other end. "Good; because they—the Prime Hunters, I mean—told me to ask you…krr-uh—they bought a lot of trade-things off the ship because they knew some of our freeholders couldn't come in for the fair. So they're holding them for resale until the latecomers arrive. We expect at least 30 or 40 more tautschen to come…"

"Churr; what *is* it, Huralen?"

"And they're asking if you can put up another five or six people for a few days—older tautschen, who like a quiet denning-place away from squealing chk-kiy-teh…*you* know, Auntie. Would that be on-stat for you?"

Would it? She looked at her new machine, dug deep inside herself for a smile, and found one.

"That would be prime, Huralen. Just send them along," she said.

C. L. Rossman lives snowed-in in NW Michigan for at least four months of the year—giving her the opportunity to write about her favorite subjects, the civilized carnivores called the tautschen or Hunters. Her stories have been published in *Crossed Genres, Golden Visions Magazine, SF Afterburn, Aiofe's Kiss, Strange, Weird & Wonderful, The Future Fire* and others. She also has three books out: *Renegade the Hunter, Renegade the Warrior,* and the latest one, *The Mission to Earth.* Look her up on Facebook or Authorsden.com.

Back To the Beginning

Marilou Goodwin

The sewer tunnels stank, and seemed to stretch on forever in enclosed infinity. I had a few inches above my head and similar inches beyond my outstretched arms, but behind me there was ten minutes straight slogging and in front of me was at least a mile before I reached my destination.

And that was *if* my directions had been right and I'd chosen the correct branches when offered the choice.

"Fuck."

The word crackled through my comm and I stopped dead. There would be no exploration, no planning the night's job, until whatever was upsetting him was fixed. He was all sorts of big on safety. If we couldn't live through it we wouldn't do it. It was the James motto, and he'd started off with the big word this time. James usually had a progression: Shit, then damn or some version of that word, *then* fuck. Starting off with the big word meant whatever had happened was serious and the job was probably off. It was certainly postponed.

Slogging through the sewage system wasn't any fun so I was chanting along with him, making the word into a litany well before I made it to the corner where I could see him again. My part in the litany was all in my head or he'd freak before I made it to him. He could curse all he wanted, but let the word slip out of my mouth and he'd go full bore into panic mode. Both of his hands were on his face and his back was to me so I stopped about 20 feet away to give the code word before getting too close to him and getting myself killed.

He turned towards me and I could see the problem right away. It helped that he was bent nearly in half to fit in the tunnel that was so well sized for me. "Fuckin' eye piece went out," he explained, as if it wasn't obvious from the black Orb in his head with the smoke leaking from it.

Moving quickly now, I walked up to him and felt his temple for the release. It was nice to not have to stretch for him for once as I reached in my pocket for the suction cup we were going to use for the job. It wasn't sterile, but it wasn't like we were putting the Orb back.

Back to the Beginning

"It'll hurt." I warned even as I protected the sensitive flesh corners of his eye as much as possible with my fingers before snatching the Orb out of his socket. I flipped it off the suction cup into the muck, hoping it hadn't messed up the suction cup too badly – we'd need it later if it would still work.

I had to hold his face to inspect the damage, elbowing his hands out of the way every two seconds as he tried to get his fingers into the empty socket. Why did men need to feel everything? "Don't touch," I warned finally, getting tired of fighting. "You don't know how much sewage you got on your hands and we don't want to have to stop everything for a few months to let you heal an infection."

Reminding him we were in the sewer seemed to work because his hands dropped to his sides, but it didn't improve his mood. "Let's go." He snarled back at me. "We're not getting this done now."

He was right. There was no way we could keep his empty socket clean while we mapped out the way. It made this trip a miserable waste of clothes, because we'd need another set to get back into the sewer later. We certainly weren't going to be able to just wash stuff we'd walked through shit in. Maybe the rubber boots could be saved at least?

We headed back to the giant grate together and pushed it open. It was one of those outlets that I couldn't imagine could have been sanitary. There'd been a river, or storm drain, or something that left a giant concrete ditch behind. Now it wasn't filled with anything but trash, and I couldn't think that it was any less sanitary in this form than it would have been with a river flowing through scooping up the shit we'd just walked through to pass on downstream.

Cursing the world and everything in it, James slammed the gate back closed and ducked out of the way. We didn't have the time to deal with the heavy chain and padlock – not if we wanted to avoid the pitiful attempts of the homeless man on the ledge above us to start the Trash River flowing again, but I grabbed the chain and swung it across the bar to make it less obvious until we got back to it.

"Watch yer aim," James shouted, bouncing up out of the concrete ditch onto the curved sides. His words were always slanged out even though I knew he had at least the standard 12th grade education chip. He hopped up again, another third of the way.

I climbed more slowly, with fewer mechanical additions. I'd been luckier in the wars, not requiring so many government-sponsored limb replacements. Usually it meant the others had to slow down to wait for me. Today, I remembered to be thankful for that luck. The natural parts might be slower but they'd never short out and shoot fire into my brain.

"I'll aim werr I wanna aim," the homeless idiot slurred, drunkenly whipping around to try to hit me with last few drops. Then James was there, his hand around the man's throat. James dangled him off the ledge while the homeless man made all the strangled sounds of fear he was able.

"James," I snapped, catching up to him. "I've been standing in piss and crap for an hour already today. A few more drops certainly won't kill me."

"Does he have an Orb?" James asked suddenly, ignoring me in favor of squinting at the dangling man's face. The man had a serious grip on James' arms and was trying to swing his legs up to catch around James' waist or get back on land or something, but he was hampered by having his pants down around his ankles.

The homeless man did his best to shake his head at James' question. It only meant he'd be out there longer since it made it harder for me to see his eyes. I gave his face a quick look as I caught up, standing beside James and leaning a little forward to look for the telltale release at the temple. "No. We're not that lucky."

"Fuck." James started to toss the man aside, but caught my tensing and tossed him for the slope instead. The man hit the ground about ten feet from us and rolled down the ramp for a few feet before he managed to stop himself and pull his pants back up. He cursed us in at least two languages, but I noticed he didn't come even a step closer and then took off rather than look at us again.

I knew it wasn't me, a smallish woman, that was scaring him, but I'd gotten used to it. My short blond hair still left me several inches short of the five and a half feet I dreamed of as a nice happy normal, even when I had it spiked up – usually when I wasn't planning on being in a sewer all day. James was my opposite. He was a giant black man with the threatening girth that worked so well on people of his particular shade, and at least four times my basic mass.

"What next?" I asked, stripping off the waterproof oversuit and folding it out to use it to help me pull off the boots without touching any exterior part. James was doing the same, but blinking a lot in the sun. I wondered if his other Orb was going out too – it would explain why I hadn't had to argue him out, and why he'd asked about the homeless man's eye instead of just knowing himself.

"James?" I started to ask about it but changed my mind. He'd hate that he'd been so obvious. Casting around for something else, I remembered his urge to steal me a doctor implant. I'd gotten my knowledge the old-fashioned way, from books and emergency technician field training, but the implant would be nice. It would give me enough extra knowledge that I hadn't nixed the idea from the get-go as I had a few others that had required killing people.

"Who put in the Orb?" I finished finally, knowing I needed some sort of question to follow his name to keep from upsetting him. The doctor who put in such a substandard device would probably be the best candidate for killing that we'd seen yet.

"He's still in Kuwait." James growled. "I thought of that too. We'll go to Miri if she's back in town."

Miri's husband had been smart enough to set aside for death insurance. She'd used it to buy a legal doctor chip. She could use it to get anywhere and make some real money, but she'd decided to stay in the slums and help the people who couldn't afford anyone else. That was sort of my dream. Not the dead husband part, she still seemed to mourn him, keeping his picture in her office and everything. But the part where she stayed where people needed her instead of moving somewhere else to give herself an easy life.

James was still working on his last boot but I started walking, knowing how often I slowed him down. He'd catch up. He always caught up. I could hear him behind me, gathering up our overalls and jumping into Trash River to get rid of them. He'd hide our boots closer, somewhere I could find. Probably just inside the grate that he'd be locking again. We had the key now, so opening it wasn't an issue any more.

He ran up behind me without the code word. If I'd done it he'd have killed me, albeit accidentally. It was trained into him so strongly it might as well have been hardwired. Him not calling wasn't forgetful or an accident though. The team all knew that I didn't need the same things. I was the pet bunny in the cage of tigers. They all loved me and one day when they killed me it would be because I'd made the mistake. They'd probably feel bad but they'd been trained differently than I had.

Not long after he caught up to me we started getting to the populated part of the city. It was the part where I knew he'd start looking for people who had an Orb – there were a lot of people around in those blocks. That meant I was looking for people with an Orb too, but I always hoped to be able to distract James so he didn't see it – ever since Richard's arm went bad and I happened be there to see him kill someone for the replacement.

It wasn't just James. It was bad any direction. If you got some equipment put in when you were in the army they weren't going to schedule another surgery to take it back, but you had to work another two years after installation to help them pay for it. They would let you leave after that though. Other armies wouldn't, but we lived in a free country and our soldiers were free to not reenlist.

The only problem was that if they didn't reenlist the government didn't feel any more responsibility for them or their mechanics, and they'd been trained to kill already. Leaving the war didn't take that proficiency away from them or give them back the emotions they'd stepped away from to be so effective over there.

They were adrift in a world with no use for them and most of them had thousands of dollars worth of equipment to keep their heart going, their ability to walk or use their arms, and it was then up to them to take care of it or fix it when it broke. Since most soldiers were also poor and struggling to find a job, at some point it just became the thing to look for someone else to take the part from. That had been the way it was long before James and I came back.

And the government had been turning a blind eye to this for decades. Soldiers who chose not to reenlist were the next best thing to deserters, and who cared when a deserter got killed in the street for a spare part? Dying in battle for your country was honorable, but leaving the battle was deserting. And never joining up in the first place? That would be one small step from treason except for the fact that the government needed them to create more soldiers.

My problem was that I was a medic more than a soldier. My height had decided my training, but I saw Miri's husband in every soldier. Someone's dad or brother and I hated the idea of killing for mechanics. But while I hated the way it worked, I also knew we didn't have money to pay for a new Orb for James and I wasn't willing to let him go.

I don't know if James took pity on me or we reached Miri's place before he saw someone, but he walked me up the stairs and ruffled my hair. That was my height too. I'd always be the kid sister to them.

"I'll go collect the team. Let them know what happened," he growled, blinking at me. He always growled. It was his natural voice so I didn't take it personally. He stumbled as he turned and stopped a minute focusing again before going on.

I winced as I watched. It wasn't entirely my height, I knew. I let them protect me. It was easier. I could see the world as a happier place than they could, and they let me. Hell, they helped me do it. If we'd have seen someone with an Orb, James would have let me distract him. He would walk away for me, no matter what it meant for him. They did so much to try to make my world something theirs had never been.

I nearly cried as James swung wide around a man with a small dog. Something in his step said he wasn't being polite as much as that he wasn't sure where the dog actually was.

I had to grow up someday, I growled at myself as I ran after him. Today was a good day for growing up, for helping James as much as he helped me. I used the safe word before I touched his arm and he jumped, not having expected me, but he didn't kill me. That was always a plus.

"You go in to see Miri. She needs to look over what I did. Make sure it's right." I did not mention looking over the other one to see if it was still working but he nodded anyway. He turned up my face to see into my eyes and I did my best to hide the misery about what I was going to have to do. Whatever he saw seemed to be good enough; he released my chin and started walking back to Miri's steps. "Be safe," he growled.

"I will." I always was. I didn't have anything to steal and I was too small to prove any man's masculinity on. I was also lucky to have the figure of a teen boy and short hair so there wasn't even any of the other fears that came with being a woman. It was a rare man who saw me that way and as far as I'd remembered it had never happened while I was walking by. In the war zone where I'd stayed in one place long enough that they might have, I'd had James to protect me.

I turned and walked before he reached the door so James couldn't catch me worrying about him. Any impression that I might think he was weak would upset him. I tried, but couldn't hear the door open and close behind me. There were enough people to hide particular sounds, but I couldn't turn back to be sure he'd made it either.

I wanted to start running – the team was still almost 2 miles away – but I didn't want to make myself look more like a victim, so I walked. I couldn't help watching faces as I went, spotting two single Orb replacements and a lot of decorative facial piercings. It felt like I should chase them down, proving my new growing up by bringing back the prize, but I was still tiny and had only ever been a medic. If I chased them down myself it was more likely our team would lose its tiny medic. Maybe not doing something dangerous could be growing up too?

The war was fought overseas, had been fought overseas for three generations, but Dallas seemed to have been an early casualty. Soldiers who didn't have anywhere else to go but weren't reenlisting were shipped back to Dallas, and most just stayed put. This had made Dallas something of an extension of the war.

In most parts of Dallas there were more ex-soldiers than anything else. People suffering post-traumatic stress were often just crazy, so it was as easy to find places in downtown Dallas riddled with bullet holes as it was in Iraq or Kuwait. Over the last ten years I'd seen three explosions where soldiers had built their own bombs in their attempts to go out with a bang. The rubble had been cleaned off the street, but the buildings had not been repaired.

Too many norms had moved away as the ex-soldiers came in and took over. Most of the money in Dallas came from taxes, and didn't go to paying any. A walk down the streets showed the difference. There were still enough people around going about their normal business that the streets were always moving, but along the building edges sat a row of dejected homeless holding out empty cups or empty hats or boxes.

If they could catch the attention of a norm they might catch enough change for a coffee or even a meal, but somehow ex-soldiers had no sympathy for other soldiers who couldn't make the grade and they were firmly ignored by most. They'd end up starving, luck into the rare honest job, or become mercs like the rest of us. That or they'd get the hell out of Dallas.

There was always a chance the rest of the world was better. I hadn't tried to find out. After the misery of the war this lesser misery of hunting ground was just right for me. Besides, going out into the real world meant risking disillusionment, and most of us would rather be miserable here because being miserable in a happy world was just too much.

Our group had taken over a bombed out building. The top three floors were missing on the south half of the building and the bottom level leaked in the rare Dallas rain since the second level floor had never been created to be waterproof – but it was all ours. We kept the good tech in the second level below ground and we lived in the first. The ground floor was kept clear of everything but traps as we used it as a blind to pull in any competition who might have decided it would be easier to off us rather than bargain against us. It was sort of like the street gangs of generations ago, but with trained military men instead.

Our team called themselves the Mongol Horde. It converted unfortunately easily into "the Mongol Whores," but we kept it anyway. We were nearly as feared as the original band. I was still two blocks away when I heard the whistled recognition sign and whistled back. They'd have gathered up to hear the news before I reached them and I could hear my comm as it was remotely clicked over to the mostly secure local link.

21

"Jess?" Ears asked as I walked up. He wasn't the big boss but he always had to know everything first. It was why we set him on the comm monitor. He'd become the voice of the group as much because he couldn't seem to stop talking as because RyAnna led with quiet confidence rather than words. "Where's James? You weren't gone long enough to finish that recon."

I almost started summarizing, but my escort arrived and I was shown through to where the others gathered. It wasn't personal; everyone was escorted in and out. Part of the security. Ears looked up impatiently from his laptop communication center, unhappy that he had to wait to hear what happened, so I started talking.

When I was finished, Ears wasted no time in patching through a secure line to Miri to check James' status. Both eyes were gone, the second short circuiting within moments of his arrival. It was better that way, she'd had time to get it out before it damaged his eye socket. Repairs to the other socket would take some time, but she was happy with the work I'd done in the field. I was thankful we'd planned on going through a window on the job so I'd had a suction cup on me.

There was a quick team discussion where Jones and Kalibri offered to be the collection team. RyAnna accepted as Ears wired up the cameras we stashed throughout the city and assigned the rest of us to a monitor. We didn't have any permanent wires because spying out allowed spying in and that wasn't an acceptable risk, but sometimes extra eyes were necessary so temporary cables were at the ready.

Eric logged in on another line to search out any military medical shipments that might run through the area in the next few days or local storage sites that might have Orbs. The best bet for uninstalled Orbs would be shipments heading to the airport, but the parts were more valuable for the military than gold. They'd run out of soldiers quick if they couldn't keep adding new parts to the mix and adding a two years to the contract for every part they replaced.

Jones and Kalibri had missed one man with a single Orb when I saw a man with two on the monitor. My chest hurt when I called it out to Ears, but there was no way my feelings were more important than James. They dropped the search quickly and started tracking the man across multiple monitors, updating Kalibri every few seconds with the coordinates.

I wandered off to my room, knowing my part was done. More than done; I was taking a role I'd never helped with before, and trying to decide whether I needed to scrub the man's face from my mind or try to burn it in permanently. Odds were he wasn't any more attached than I was. This was an ex town, after all, and he was probably someone just home from war without anywhere better to go. Still didn't make me feel any better about marking him for death.

My roommate, Lori, hugged me as I walked in. I had a hard time figuring out how she fit in the group, but she seemed harmless. She was the mother-figure if nothing else. Ours wasn't exactly the most normal relationship, but then James and I had been teamed up for most of our service time and all our time back and I couldn't seem to find that trust for anyone else. We worked well together. The fact that I was tiny seemed to go well with him being giant and left us open for jobs on both ends of the spectrum.

I ignored her, flipping through my books looking for more information on eyes and Orbs. I could find eyes but Orbs came after everything went digital. I'd have to ask for clearance, but the lines were busy on something else right now. Off-duty, due to the failed job, I could certainly wait. Instead, I picked up the book about the initial limb replacements and started reading again. Patience was not natural to me. Lori smiled and went back to her knitting. She called it her stress relief. Every now and then I thought I should try it, but I was pretty sure you it wouldn't work for me.

It wasn't too long before I heard the muffled cheer from downstairs but I was pretty sure it was a cheer for acquiring the Orbs rather than getting them to James. Knowing how they were acquired, I couldn't quite cheer for it myself. I cheered for James living instead. Ears was on my comm before I could settle back into my book, asking if I wanted to come down and scan for chips or if they should have Jerry take care of it.

What could I say, I went down to scan. Jerry wasn't as thorough as I was and occasionally missed things. To prove the point, he scowled at me as I walked into our makeshift operating room. "I can tell by looking at this one he's not mech'ed out. He's probably not even a soldier. No scars at all," Jerry sniffed, stalking out. When I found something he would claim that I'd kicked him out and didn't give him any time. It had happened before, but everyone knew so it wasn't an issue. That was why Ears had called me, after all.

Because something else had to be there. No one ran around with Orbs and nothing else. If he was a soldier he'd at least have a titanium skull plate because the eyes would have been replaced due to damage. Jerry couldn't handle cutting either, so with him there alone, the team had only had basic first aid before I'd arrived. I hated killing, but cutting up the dead was just practical. Who had the money to let thousands of dollars rot out of respect for an empty corpse?

I flashed on the rumor that the military had begun starting off with replacement parts in an attempt to create a sort of super-soldier, but pushed it aside. Who would willingly sign up for chopping off perfectly good body parts to install something that had a 30% chance of failure right up front and a small but definite chance of circuit failure frying your brain any time afterwards?

Jerry had already pulled the eyes for Miri. Maybe earlier the cheer had been for getting the Orbs out whole. The scanner readings were close enough to normal that Jerry would have signed him off already, but they weren't quite right. I pulled out my scalpel for testing and scraped across the skin on his wrist.

Faux-skin. They were getting better at it all the time. I grabbed a wooden ruler and scraped it up the arm, watching closely for the tiny crease, feeling for the small thump that would show the end of the faux skin and the beginning of real skin. It felt like real skin and moved like real skin but there had to be a join somewhere. As far as I knew they still couldn't program equal to a brain, but I was nearly to the shoulder when I found it set above one joint and below another to minimize the rubbing. We didn't have anyone needing full arm in our team, but we could easily trade it to Miri for services. She could sell the ones we didn't need to the next person who came in.

I dribbled the glue remover along the nearly invisible seam and pried it away from the dead flesh, scraping out the bits that tore and detaching it from the internal controls. I'd have to pull them out later along with the balloon they added into living muscle to help with pressure sensing. Those balloons were more valuable than the arm itself.

Then I tested the contact points to see it work before letting Ears know he had it to use it for bargaining. He chuckled happily as I started checking the other side. Our corspe had two full arms and two full legs mech'ed out, making those rumors about purposeful replacements seem a little more likely and making Jerry a fucking moron for not catching any of this. Ears vocalized my thoughts when I called it in.

I wondered what the collectors had done to get the drop on someone like this – he had to have had sense enhancers installed with the Orbs, though I wouldn't see them until I started cutting. They were so delicate I never tried to get them out myself. Still, even Kalibri wasn't good enough to grab this much tech without some serious luck.

Not that that meant much to the person tasked with pulling him apart. It was a lot of work, but finally all the removable mech was detached and sitting aside. I was down to torso and head to continue discovery on before I started opening him up for the rest of the goodies. With all the peripheral mechanics, there had to be something amazing inside.

Switching to the metal detector, I could see that his entire skull was plated and it looked like they were doing something new with the ribcage. I wouldn't know if they'd figured out a way to plate that too or had done some sort of pin until I started cutting. Kalibri would be after me to melt it down though, when he found out it was here. He kept a supply of metal until they found me a chip so I could install it. I hoped they knew it took more than just the basic doctor chip to do that, and a real operating room. We'd have to find ourselves a budget before I'd operate on anyone that we wanted to keep alive.

Each discovery was made it more likely this ex would be little more than a mushy scrapheap once I'd finished with him. Especially after I pulled on some gloves and started making incisions along the base of his skull, the first actual cutting I'd done on him. I felt along the edge and found six different chips and a GPS tracker. While one was easily the required K – 12 Ed-Chip, there were five I had no clue about, and the last was a beacon to bring people to us and the body.

I commed Ears again, cursing roundly because I could with him, and let him know that not only did we have a treasure trove of goodies with this guy, we were also seriously fucked. This guy was way too young to have served out all the years these upgrades would have cost so we'd apparently just killed a brand new super soldier who'd been sent to our hometown rather than the war zone. And he had a tracker leading anyone following him straight to me.

Back to the Beginning

I felt every second tick by as Ears sent Kalibri in to collect the chip and walk it away. We hoped it would make it less obvious that something had happened here. Kalibri grinned at seeing the company's most vocal pacifist covered in blood, but when I was cutting I was in a different world and I didn't have time to deal with him.

The corpse had titanium coated ribs, something I'd never seen on the small bones before, and his heart was mechanical, but the rest of his insides were soft. I scooped them out to check, dropping them one by one into the waste barrel for processing. We weren't really set up to collect soft parts yet and my explorations ruined them anyway. He had two livers. I'd never seen that before so I made a mental note to ask Miri about it later.

"We really need to get that Listener into the Gov system," Ears said softly in the comm. It was the voice he used when he didn't want to say outright that he was talking only to me or that I shouldn't spread this information around. It wasn't necessary since he was talking about our aborted morning mission but it was appreciated anyway. We hadn't let that mission be full knowledge since the size of our team almost guaranteed a mole. We'd just topped fifty, and our groups were working with the best of military efficiency.

"It's even more important now," he continued, "so we can find out about that guy."

"We can't while James is laid up." I was running the intestines through my hands searching for hard spots or something that might be hidden there. "We work too well together. I can't go with anyone else. We did the prep work together."

"He's out already." Ears replied. "You've been with that ex a while."

Guts were a much better time sink than the books, I thought sadly, wondering what to say to Ears as I sliced open the intestine to find the lumps inside. Another two chips had been sewn into the lining in a fancy little flesh pouch to keep them safe.

"Fuck." I went straight to James' big word, then said it twice more. The corpse had been a courier. Hell was going to rain down on us, and if Hell, for some reason, didn't know it was us it might just rain down on all of Dallas. It wouldn't be the first time the city had been cleansed.

I hadn't realized I'd said it aloud until Ears asked for clarification. I sighed with the explanation and kept sorting internals. "When I finish this, if James is feeling up to it, we'll go back. We'll go back tonight, in the dark, if we need to."

"Should I send Jerry in to help?" Ears started, then changed course. "James' ETA is 30 minutes."

"No to Jerry. He really should have seen something on this guy. But send James on in when he gets here. We'll talk while I finish and decide if the security we know of will work as well at night, make sure we're not after the janitors to the point we'll trip the motion sensors. I don't even know what time it is any more but the good news is the sewers can't get any darker."

Ears laughed and my comm went silent. He'd probably gone to talk James

Marilou Goodwin

into it if he needed to. I wished I could tell James it wasn't important and we could wait till he was better but this guy made my skin crawl. What a bitch if we'd saved James' eyes only to kill us all. And what was wrong with Jerry anyway?

When I flipped the corpse, I found the knife wound low in his back. Kalibri had probably gotten him in the street, not even bothering to lure him anywhere. A subtle stabbing, disguised as a manly greeting, then walking him off like some drunk friend.

The corpse's spine had been coated too, for what little good it did. We were so fucked. This guy alone cost the government millions and that wasn't even including the information on the intestine chips or the ones from his skull.

Terror made me fast and I'd just gotten clean when James strolled in, looking as awake and healthy as ever except for the small rips at the corners of his eyes. My side was a little larger than Miri's but mine was done in the field and in the dark, so I wasn't going to take it too hard. Miri's were probably scalpel cuts rather than rips too, but all in all it wasn't too bad. They had a light coating of some antibacterial gel on them. I reached up to touch the tear for a second, safe since I was approaching from the front and he watched me the whole way. He ducked his head for me to see better before capturing my hand.

"If we're going back into sewers you should wear goggles." I told him, wiping gel on my new clean pants. He was still covered.

He nodded and collected a pair. Ears had another set of gear ready for us and James grabbed the bag on our way out. It was dusk before we'd made it back to the giant grate, before we'd pulled on the new waterproof overalls and collected our boots. Soon we were back inside, splitting at the fork to check a possible alternate escape that was mapped to join back up with my tunnel about three quarters of a mile away. We were on our way. It was the same path – just hours later. Hopefully we'd find the right spot and get the Listener installed. Maybe that way we'd at least get a warning before death came hunting.

The sewer tunnels stank and seemed to stretch on forever in enclosed infinity. I had a few inches above my head and similar inches beyond my outstretched arms, but behind me there was ten minutes straight slogging and in front of me was at least a mile before I reached my destination. There was hope in James' continued silence.

Marilou Goodwin spends her real-life time in Florida with her laptop, her two children, and her husband – possibly in that order, says the husband. She spends her online time as Clothdragon. See more from Marilou at http://clothdragon.blogspot.com/.

A Crazy Kind of Love

Jeremy Zimmerman

"It's a shame we can't have umbrellas," Bran commented miserably, his dark hair plastered around his head as rivulets of rainwater streamed down over him. He pulled his cloak around him tighter in hopes that it might become more waterproof.

"It's a shame the gra'al react poorly to them," Imogen said through a forced smile plastered on her face. Her sound of contrived joy made her sound almost as though she were singing. "And this is all about making the gra'al happy."

The two of them stood in a circle of fluted marble pillars around a dais of the same material. An archway stood at one end of the circle. Rain came down in a torrent, making the pillars only faintly visible in the gloom. The dais did not drain water very efficiently, leaving pools of water standing on the surface.

"You know, I don't see why you're holding that smile already," Bran said. "We don't even know when the ambassador will arrive."

"Because if I drop the smile," Imogen answered as she pushed a sodden golden lock out of her face, "I might start crying. Do you have the scroll with the speech on it handy?"

Sniffling, Bran replied, "Yes. It's still sealed up but it's just inside my coat."

"Good man," Imogen replied. "All those years of education have clearly paid off for you," she jibed in her trilling tones of mock joy.

Bran coughed and said, "Imogen, if you're going to be a bitch, I can just leave you behind next time."

"Promises, promises," she said in lilting tones.

A light flickered in the archway, catching the pair's attention. It flickered a few times before resolving into a brilliant glow, cutting through the gloom. Imogen cleared her throat. Bran straightened up and peered forward expectantly, the misery of the cold and wet forgotten for the moment.

The gra'al's first two legs came through first, chitinous limbs probing through the arch for footing. Its tarsi tapped hesitantly down on the marble before the next pair of legs came through with the bulk of the gra'al's form. The tentacles around its oral disk drifted as though caught in a current that the humans present could not feel.

As it pulled its bulk the rest of the way through the portal, the slight form of a human woman followed behind it. The woman moved cautiously, as though having trouble with balance. She was dressed in nothing more than a thin, simple dress that was instantly soaked through in the downpour. As the gra'al came to a halt in front of the trio, the woman walked gingerly around the gra'al and rested her hand amongst its tentacles. At the shoulder the gra'al was a foot taller than the woman, not including the writhing mass of boneless limbs that stretched upwards from the top of its carapace.

Imogen held a hand towards Bran who opened the scroll case, slid out the scroll within and passed it to her. After handing it off, Bran unshuttered a lantern for her to see by.

"Ambassador T'k'l'k of the Gra'al League, and Speaker Belinda, we are honored to have your presence return to our humble kingdom. We bear with us the words of our monarch, King Gwalch—"

"This one appreciates your desire to properly welcome us," the woman interrupted in a tired and fragile voice. "But this one has had a taxing journey and, while this one would not want to create a diplomatic incident, this one would really prefer to settle back into this one's accommodations."

Imogen's face had frozen with her mouth open in mid-speech. After a moment she managed to adapt to the sudden change and said brightly, "Of course, of course. Please, this way. We have your transportation just down the hill. We should be happy to transport you back to your consulate."

The two led the ambassador and its speaker down to where a pair of carriages awaited. T'k'l'k's carriage could only barely be considered such, and was much more like a well decorated wagon. After ensuring that the ambassador and Belinda were securely seated in the wagon, Bran and Imogen entered their own carriage to finally get out of the rain.

Once the carriages began moving, Imogen covered her mouth with the edge of her cloak and screamed into it.

Bran, slumped in the opposite corner of the carriage, noted dryly, "Your perpetual grace always astounds me."

"Two hours!" she exclaimed.

"It's hard to coordinate schedules between our world and theirs," Bran said, mostly to himself since it was clear Imogen wasn't listening.

"In the rain!" she continued.

"They don't control the weather," he muttered.

"And then it turns out our entire little welcoming ceremony was unnecessary!" she fumed.

"You know, Imogen, if it upsets you so much," Bran commented, focusing his attention on the rain that fell outside the carriage, "You could get another assignment within the diplomatic branch. I think it's understood that not everyone has what it takes to work as a liaison to extradimensional entities."

"No, no," she assured him tersely. "I'm just venting a little. While I don't come at this as a labor of love like you do, I recognize the importance of this work. The supplies of thaumium they provide us are invaluable and it's important to maintain good relations."

"And it looks good on your service record," Bran muttered darkly.

"That," Imogen huffed, "is just a side benefit."

"Okay," Bran said, hoping to convey that he was done with the conversation.

Imogen did not discuss the subject further for the rest of the ride, except to occasionally mutter "two hours" and "in the rain."

*

It was still raining the following morning. Bran, seated in the smaller private dining room, still sniffled occasionally as he reviewed a stack of parchments while eating breakfast. His reports to his superior, Lord Cai, seemed never-ending. He could not believe the maintenance of this diplomatic outpost required so much minutiae.

He heard a shuffling of bare feet on the rug and glanced up to see Speaker Belinda moving carefully into the room. She still wore the same shapeless gown and nothing else. Her white hair, now dry, was frizzy and unkempt.

Standing hastily, he bowed slightly and said, "Good morning, Speaker Belinda. I hadn—"

"Please," she interrupted as she moved carefully to one of the chairs, "no fuss. This is not an official meeting. I just wanted to apologize for our abruptness last night."

"Not necess—" Bran started to say, but she raised her hand to interrupt him again as she sat down gingerly.

"Do let me finish," she pleaded softly. When Bran did not begin talking again, she continued, "Ambassador T'k'l'k was mainly accommodating me in his desire to skip formalities. While the gra'al are notorious sticklers for procedure, their... fondness for their Speakers often circumvents their normal inclinations. I have not been well." She hesitated before adding, "To be more precise, I am dying."

Bran started to say something, but she wearily raised a hand again. "It is a result of the process which allows a human to bond with a gra'al in order to become a Speaker. I knew when I agreed to it that it would hasten my end. While I am saddened to see my time with T'k'l'k end, I do not for a moment regret my choice. So please, no words of sympathy."

Bran raised a hand.

"Yes?" she asked.

"May I ask a question?" Bran asked. She chuckled and nodded, and so he continued by inquiring, "While I am honored at your confidence, may I ask what your ultimate purpose in telling me all this is?"

"The Ambassador curtailed his visit home in order to seek out my replacement," Belinda explained. "It was hoping to discuss the logistics of such a search with you tonight. Perhaps over dinner?"

"Of course, I'll let Imogen know when she arrives for breakfast and... You're shaking your head. Am I missing something?" Bran asked.

"T'k'l'k was hoping to meet with you privately," the Speaker explained. She hurried to add, "While we certainly respect Imogen's qualities as a member of His Majesty's diplomatic force, you have spent several years working with the Gra'al League in general and T'k'l'k in particular. T'k'l'k feels you could better appreciate the delicacy of the situation than your cohort, and as such it feels it can be more... frank in conversing with you than it might be with Imogen present."

Bran blinked a few times in surprise and then shrugged slightly, saying, "Very well. Shall I meet you at the main dining room around the ninth bell?"

"That sounds excellent," the Speaker said, giving a pained smile as she slowly rose to her feet. "We will see you then."

As she gingerly walked towards the door she nearly ran into Imogen who, though dressed, was moving bleary eyed into the dining room and paying little attention to where she was going. They made faint noises of apology to one another and each continued on their way.

"Well," Imogen commented, "she's up bright and early."

"Mm-hm," Bran agreed. "She wanted to invite me to dinner with the ambassador. Don't worry, you're off the hook. It just wanted to meet with me."

"Good," Imogen said as she sat down and, after checking the contents of the teapot, poured herself a cup of tea. "The last thing I need is another bout of watching someone hand-feed a gra'al. Eegh." She punctuated her noise of disgust by shuddering, scrunching up her face and briefly flailing her hands.

"Ah, ever the professional," Bran smirked as he went back to his work.

*

The main 'dining room' was less of a room and more of an open courtyard. This served to accommodate both the gra'al dislike of being separated from the elements and the practical need to give their poisoned tentacles room to move freely. It was primarily reserved for more formal functions involving the gra'al, since the human residents preferred more hospitable environs.

There were two tables in the courtyard. One had a chair seated before it and a normal looking meal waiting. The other had an assortment of whole fish laid out on it, with no chairs nearby.

Bran entered the courtyard, dressed in some of his finer clothes. He glanced apprehensively at the sky. Most of his budget was spent on replacing finery damaged by the torrential rains of the region, and he was not looking forward to spending another night soaked to the bone.

He lingered near his table, not yet sitting, watching for the door through which the gra'al and its Speaker would arrive. After a few minutes, the entity entered, gracefully negotiating down the steps with Speaker Belinda, coming to a halt at the seafood-laden table.

Bran bowed respectfully; Belinda returned the bow. T'k'l'k also crouched slightly, the gra'al equivalent of a bow or curtsey. As Bran sat in his chair, the Ambassador and the Speaker had a moment of silent communion. After a minute the Speaker walked over and selected one of the fish, stumbled slightly under the weight as she lifted it and held it up to the gra'al's tentacles. T'k'l'k snatched the food in its tentacles, slowly drawing the fish into its mouth. Belinda repeated the effort a few times before stopping, her chest heaving from the effort, and resting her hand among the tendrils. She turned to Bran, who had long since begun enjoying his meal.

"This one thanks you for humoring this one," the Speaker said on behalf of the gra'al.

"I assure you," Bran said after swallowing a bite, "that, as a representative of His Majesty King Gwalchmai, I am honored to meet with you at any time."

"This one wonders what your personal feelings are on the matter."

Bran paused, surprised at the question. The gra'al were usually formal and aloof. After a moment he said, "I have long enjoyed our conversations in the past, Ambassador. As such, I am happy to spend time with you tonight."

There was a pause, the Speaker slipping out of her role of neutral expression of the Ambassador's will as she looked at T'k'l'k questioningly. Bran assumed it was a moment of silent communion, but he wasn't entirely sure.

Belinda frowned slightly at the gra'al before turning to Bran and conveying, "This one wonders if you are merely flattering this one. An honest answer would be appreciated."

Still thrown off guard, Bran cautiously said, "I assure you that I am not merely humoring you. I have had many opportunities to transfer to another post, but I have remained at this one due to my... high regard for the gra'al."

"High regard?" the Speaker asked, and Bran found himself for once uncertain whether the question came ultimately from the Speaker or the Ambassador. "Could you elaborate?"

Bran pursed his lips for a few moments before deciding on frankness; "The gra'al fascinate me. I became interested in the diplomatic branch because I am intrigued by those who are different from myself, and there are none as different as the gra'al."

Belinda turned to regard T'k'l'k, communing briefly with the gra'al before turning back to Bran and saying, "This one wonders how you would feel if given the opportunity to visit the gra'al world."

"I would of course be delighted by the opportunity," Bran said hesitantly. "But it is my understanding that the world is not very hospitable to humans."

"There is a way to work around that limitation," the Speaker noted.

"You mean the Speaker initiation," Bran stated, not as a question. The Speaker nodded.

With sudden comprehension, Bran asked, "You asked me here to see if I would replace Belinda?"

The Speaker flicked a brief glance at the gra'al before nodding.

Bran's heart fluttered. This was so far away from text-book interaction with the gra'al that he was certain he was going to screw this up. The Speaker regarded him coolly, perhaps sensing his need to process this.

T'k'l'k adjusted its footing frequently, even though the movement was unnecessary, and rubbed its pedipalps together. Bran did not want to consider the possibility of a gra'al fidgeting.

"I would think you would want to have a wide array of candidates to select from," Bran noted uncertainly.

"Few are acquainted with the gra'al on any level, and fewer still are those acquainted with the gra'al and yet feel comfortable around them. The role of Speaker should not be misconstrued as merely a glorified translator position. It represents a significant bond between Speaker and gra'al."

"How significant?" Bran asked.

"Some have described it as being more intimate than marriage. Though most humans only see the expression of the gra'al through the Speaker, the empathic bond is a two-way experience."

Bran laughed nervously, taking a few bites of food to stall for time. Perhaps intuiting his need to absorb this, the Speaker went over and pulled another fish from the table and offered it up to the gra'al.

After swallowing, Bran asked, "In light of this information, I cannot help but wonder: Why me?"

"This one has enjoyed working with you during this one's time as ambassador. This one has high regard for your skills and professionalism. Plus—" at this point the Speaker broke off and whipped her head around to stare in mild surprise at the gra'al. A quiet time of communion passed between them. Bran had never seen such behavior before, but he suspected that the Speaker and the Ambassador were arguing.

Bran took another bite of food just as Belinda and T'k'l'k seemed to come to a resolution. Belinda had a dubious expression on her face, but that soon faded as she slipped back into the role of Speaker.

"This one also thinks you are pretty," she said for the gra'al.

Bran nearly choked on the bite of food he was eating. He drank a long swallow of wine in order to clear his throat. "Pretty?" Bran asked in confusion.

"Yes. This one hopes that this one did not offend you or overstep the boundaries of proper decorum."

"No, no, not offended," Bran said. "I've been called many things in my time, but 'pretty' has never been one of them."

Silence reigned for a few minutes.

"This one is certain you must have many questions," the Speaker prompted.

"Yes, but I don't yet know what most of them are," Bran admitted. He hesitated before saying, "I do have one, however: Is its interest sexual?"

"Is that an issue for you?"

He pursed his lips, as though savoring the words in his mouth before saying, "No, I just want to know what I'm getting into."

"No, it is not sexual. The gra'al derive no significant pleasure from sexual stimulation, especially from humans. The transformation into a Speaker also diminishes libido, but the bond more than compensates for the lack of physical intimacy. Aesthetics influence this one's decision, but personality is also a significant contributor."

"Oh," Bran said, pausing before adding, "I will need time to think on this. How soon do you need an answer?"

"The process cannot begin while Speaker Belinda is alive, but she will also not be able to answer questions once she is gone. After her passing, this one will not want to be without a Speaker for very long."

"That's... a nebulous time frame," Bran pointed out.

"This one apologizes for that."

*

"I can't believe you're seriously considering this," Imogen spat out.

She'd been having a glass of wine in a sitting room when Bran came to fill her in on the meeting. Given her tipsy state, it may not have been her first glass.

"It's an amazing opportunity," Bran said tiredly, already tired of this conversation.

"An amazing opportunity to spend your time filthy and half naked on some alien world," she countered, "with the promise of an early grave."

"It's a chance to experience another culture vastly different from our own," he sighed.

"This isn't a summer across the sea, learning another language and eating exotic food," Imogen yelled. "This is spending the rest of your suddenly shortened life playing love slave to a *thing*." To emphasize the last, she held a hand up to her forehead and wiggled her fingers to emulate the gra'al tentacles.

"It's not sexual," Bran emphasized, wearily massaging the bridge of his nose.

"Oh, I'm sure that's what they tell you up front," Imogen said with a dismissive wave of her hand, sloshing the wine in her glass. "And then next thing you know you're up to your elbows in sensual oils providing—" She shuddered rather than finish that thought.

"Are you speaking from your own personal experience?" Bran jibed.

Imogen leveled an annoyed glare at him in return and firmly replied, "No."

Neither said anything further. Finally, Bran made his excuses and went off to bed.

*

33

It was a clear and sunny day when Bran woke late the next morning. He knew the bright sky lent a false hope. Without the insulating cloud layer, the day would be bone-chillingly cold outside.

The servants had thoughtfully stoked the fire in his hearth, so his room was comfortable as he pulled away the bedding and shuffled sleepily over to the wash basin to splash water on his face. As he blinked away the water, he noticed a piece of paper that had been slipped under his door.

He picked it up and quickly recognized the Speaker's stiff, awkward handwriting. The note read, "The Ambassador would like to invite you to join it on a walk at your convenience."

Bran slowly got dressed as his brain gradually woke up. He picked out a few layers of shirts and coats so that he could remove or add layers depending on the vagaries of the weather. On his way to the Ambassador's quarters he swung by the kitchen to grab some bread and cheese to function as a breakfast.

Like many of the accommodations in place for gra'al, the Ambassador's quarters were a series of linked courtyards left open to the elements. Bran approached the main door and tugged on the bell pull.

A few minutes later Speaker Belinda opened the door and welcomed him in. She stank of fish. "The Ambassador was just finishing breakfast," she explained. "I'll bring it out in just a moment."

Bran waited idly in the courtyard, nibbling on his bread and cheese, occasionally swinging his arms and bending at the knees to keep the blood flowing. After ten minutes T'k'l'k came out, its tarsi tapping across the flagstones of the courtyard.

In the years that he had worked this post, Bran had never seen a gra'al under direct sunlight. They mostly kept to themselves during the day, and so he had only ever seen them under cloud cover or by firelight. The bright light brought out subtle variations in color across the Ambassador's exoskeleton and lent a crystalline quality to its translucent tentacles.

The Speaker was leaning wearily against the doorway, a tired smile on her face. "You two have fun," she said softly. "T'k'l'k, don't wear out Bran."

Bran froze in alarm. After a moment, panic let go of his tongue and he asked in a higher pitched voice, "Are you not coming?"

"No," she said. "I am very tired today and you two need some time to bond."

"But... how do we talk?" Bran asked, his fear not diminishing.

"T'k'l'k can understand you if you talk," she explained. "It just won't be able to talk back."

"Anything else I should know?" Bran asked anxiously.

"Don't forget that the tentacles are poisonous to humans," she pointed out. "Otherwise you're fine touching it anywhere else."

Bran turned to the Ambassador and awkwardly said, "Shall we?"

*

A Crazy Kind of Love

The walk helped Bran warm up, allowing him to take off his overcoat and carry it draped over his arm. T'k'l'k strode purposefully at his side, its segmented legs gracefully picking their way along the trail.

Occasionally the Ambassador would stop and seem to examine something: mushrooms, a tree, a large rock. There was little warning when the gra'al decided to look at something, often leaving Bran several steps ahead before he noticed he was alone. Bran understood that the gra'al could see, but he was never clear on how that functioned.

"That's quite a tree," Bran said out of the blue, hoping to make a little conversation even if it was doomed to being one-sided.

The gra'al shifted slightly, its attention seeming to be focused on Bran.

"I wish I knew more about trees," Bran said. "Some of the embassy staff are familiar with the woods out here and can tell you about every flower and mushroom and bird and tree. Unfortunately for you, you picked the man who studied foreign cultures and languages."

The Ambassador's attention didn't shift from Bran.

"Did you want to resume walking?" Bran offered.

T'k'l'k cautiously maneuvered back to the trail and continued onward.

"It's a beautiful day," Bran said after a few minutes of walking. "We don't often get sunny days this time of year. I can never decide if it's better or worse than the constant rain."

The gra'al halted again, this time to examine a large rock. Bran noticed the stop more quickly this time and was able to more quickly join the gra'al in observation of the stone. Without entirely thinking about it, he casually rested a hand on one of the gra'al's legs.

The gra'al backed up unexpectedly and turned, forcing Bran to backpedal hurriedly. As it turned to face Bran, the diplomat realized that the gra'al had a flower clutched awkwardly in its pedipalps.

*

"This must be what hell feels like," Bran thought to himself the next morning as he lay in bed. Despite injunctions by Belinda, T'k'l'k did wear him out. Bran did not normally walk that much, and he could already feel vestigial blisters blossoming across his feet while muscles he thought he hadn't even used hurt.

He awoke to find another note from Belinda slipped under his door, inviting him to another walk. He wearily wrote back explaining that he needed some time to recover and would try to join them for supper.

Stiffly, he walked down to the private dining room and stared blankly at the table while servants brought out breakfast.

Footsteps could be heard moving stridently down the hall. Bran looked slowly up, mentally preparing himself for Imogen. He was surprised to see the stout form of his superior, Lord Cai, bustle into the room.

The senior diplomat looked rumpled. His clothing was creased and his hair was mussed, implying that he had slept in those clothes and had not been able to make himself more presentable.

Bran stood up hurriedly, pain stretching across his thighs and causing him to wince. He bowed slightly to his superior and waited for Lord Cai to sit before returning to his own seat. Bran noted with a frown that Lord Cai made a point of waiting for the servants to leave and closing the door behind them before sitting.

"My lord, it's a pleasant surprise to see you here," Bran said stiffly.

"It is pleasant to see you as well," Lord Cai said. "I wish that my reason for visiting was under the mantle of more pleasant circumstances."

"You say that as though something is wrong," Bran prompted.

"Yesterday morning, I received a letter from Miss Imogen, expressing in no uncertain terms her concern regarding you," Lord Cai said matter-of-factly. "She seemed to believe you were considering becoming involved in some strange relationship with the Ambassador."

Bran pursed his lips as he realized that Imogen must have immediately sent that letter after talking to him, having a messenger ride post to get it to the city by morning.

"I have been offered the opportunity to become a Speaker for the Ambassador," Bran explained flatly. "Speaker Belinda is in declining health and Ambassador T'k'l'k is looking for another Speaker. Given our good working relations over the past several years, the Ambassador was inclined to offer me the position."

Lord Cai frowned and said, "Miss Imogen's letter implied there was something a bit more lurid involved."

"The process in becoming a Speaker seems to create a close psychic bond with the gra'al in question, lending a certain level of intimacy," the younger diplomat said, pointedly leaving out such things as the Ambassador's fondness for his looks. "Imogen was not willing to believe there was not some nefarious secret aspect to this bond."

"But surely you realize that you cannot be certain what this gra'al's ultimate intentions are towards you," Bran's superior huffed. "Not to mention that it is, effectively, a death sentence for you to take the position."

"Both valid points," Bran admitted guardedly, not wanting to get into an argument on the subject.

"You're thinking of going through with this, aren't you?" Lord Cai accused.

"I am keeping my options open," Bran said, trying to remain impassive.

"I have been quite busy seeking out opinions on the subject," the elder diplomat said as he reached for the satchel he had brought in. "I did, of course, also contact your family." At those words, Bran rolled his eyes. "Your mother is quite beside herself with dismay. I have letters from several in your family for you to read here. There is also the concern from the intelligence division that by forming this bond you may be in a position to reveal state secrets."

"I've been working at this outpost for years," Bran pointed out with a sigh.

"I don't have any state secrets. There is nothing that I've had contact with except gra'al."

"Don't sell yourself short," Lord Cai said dismissively. "You know a good deal of the functioning of the diplomatic branch. We cannot simply let that information out to anyone."

"With all due respect," Bran sighed again, "I think you're rationalizing."

"I do not agree, but I will not push the point further," Lord Cai said with a note of sympathy. "But the Crown does have an alternative they would like to propose."

"I'm all ears," Bran said flatly.

Laying his hands flat on the table and regarding them, Lord Cai said, "The Crown does not appreciate the bottleneck formed by the gra'al monopoly on thaumium. It would be advantageous to the Crown if we were able to take steps to loosen that hold."

"I'm not sure if I understand your meaning," Bran replied.

"If you were to gather intelligence for us in order for us to remove the gra'al from the picture..." Lord Cai prompted.

"No."

The senior diplomat looked up in faint surprise and said, "Your King needs you."

"Not that badly," Bran stated.

Lord Cai shook his head and said, "Then you force my hand. You are under house arrest and will be prohibited access to the Ambassador. Once I can arrange the proper accommodations, you will be transferred back to the city."

*

No further discussion was allowed. Lord Cai had brought a trio of soldiers from the city and they had been assigned the task of keeping Bran away from the Ambassador. Bran had spent the day pacing up and down the length of his room, his anger coiling tightly in his chest.

Towards evening a knock came at his door. He debated whether to answer and during his indecision the door opened. Imogen stepped through holding a dinner tray.

She looked sheepishly at him and commented, "I thought that if I was holding your food you'd be less inclined to hit me."

"Don't sell yourself short," Bran shot back. "Being hittable is one of your strong suits."

She pushed back against the door to close it, and then walked over to a table in Bran's room to set down his food. "I didn't know they'd do all this," she said in a low tone, quietly regarding the plates on the tray.

"That's not much of a defense," he retorted.

"It's about all I've got," she offered lamely. "I know we don't usually get along, but I couldn't just watch you destroy yourself. I'm not *that* callous."

Bran made a noncommittal grunt in response, not willing to acknowledge any vaguely positive quality she might have.

"You didn't really want to do the whole Speaker thing, anyway, did you?" she prompted.

"How often have you felt wanted?" he asked her.

"Well," she said with a smirk, "I don't mean to brag, but—"

"I mean wanted for being you," Bran interrupted. "Not just because you might represent some trophy to be gained in a night but because someone looked at you and realized that you were the person they wanted in their life?"

"Okay," she shrugged. "You got me there. So you're saying you want to leave your family behind and destroy your health because you feel validated?"

"I'm not saying that's all there is to it," he said. "But that's a factor. I've worked here for years, fascinated by the gra'al and wanting to learn more and now, suddenly, one of them has asked me to be a permanent fixture in its life. How do I just walk away from that?"

"I've got a smart-ass answer for that, but I think I'll save that for another time," she dryly.

"Did you come here just to offer half-ass apologies and smart-ass comments?" he asked as he walked over to review the contents of his dinner tray. "Or did you want to help me get out?"

"What exactly are you proposing?" she asked warily.

*

The guard looked over when he heard the door open, and was startled to see an enraged Bran standing behind a wide-eyed Imogen, with one hand holding her by a fist-full of hair, the other hand holding a dinner knife to her throat.

"Just back away from the door and she doesn't get hurt," Bran instructed through clenched teeth.

The guard stepped slowly away and Bran maneuvered himself and his hostage through the door, keeping his eyes on the guard as they slowly backed down the hall.

Once out of earshot of the guard, Imogen whispered, "Could you be more careful with that knife? I think you nicked me."

"Now is not the time, Imogen," Bran whispered back tersely.

"You are notoriously clumsy," he pointed out. "I should have thought of that before I agreed to this scheme."

Bran might have had further input, but Lord Cai's voice rang out down the hall, "Bran, what the hell do you think you're doing?"

Bran and, more cautiously, Imogen turned to look down the hall where Lord Cai was standing.

"I'm affecting an escape," Bran shot back, punctuating his statement with a tug of Imogen's hair. Imogen let out a yelp of pain.

"I was on my way to see you," Lord Cai said, shaking his head. "I met with

T'k'l'k to let it know of the change in staffing. The Ambassador decided to leave then and there in what I can only describe as 'a huff.' It made vague threats of trade sanctions for our so-called 'effrontery.' I had hoped that you might have come to your senses and would be willing to at least talk down the Ambassador, but I hardly expected you to be engaged in such... absurdities."

"The Ambassador is gone?" Bran asked, his grip on Imogen loosening. The senior diplomat nodded and Bran followed up with, "Headed towards the gate?"

As soon as Lord Cai nodded in response to the second question, Bran had let go of Imogen and went running down the hall past his superior, the stiff muscles in his legs screaming in agony at the exertion. Bran heard Lord Cai call after him, but he ignored the lord as he went running out a service door and into the night.

*

He found the Ambassador and the Speaker to the side of the road on the way to the gate that led to the gra'al's world. A light mist filled the air, not quite rain but by no means dry. Belinda was leaning against a tree, looking even more pale than normal, while T'k'l'k shifted its legs about in an agitated fashion, its pedipalps rubbing together briskly and even its tentacles thrashing about anxiously.

Bran had long since had to give up on running. He'd made it out past the boundaries of the diplomatic outpost before his stamina gave up on him. He had managed to catch his breath, but still coughed infrequently.

As he came upon the gra'al and its Speaker, Belinda looked up wearily. A few moments later, the gra'al turned and looked at Bran, its agitation seeming to intensify briefly before it seemed to calm down.

Stiffly, Bran walked over and dropped awkwardly into a seated position on the grass next to Belinda. T'k'l'k sidled over and Bran reached out a hand to affectionately rub one of the gra'al's legs. "This went badly," Bran commented, punctuating his statement with a cough.

Belinda nodded wearily and said in a quiet tone, "If the gra'al had a holy book, it would mostly consist of variations on, 'Act in haste, repent in leisure.' After we learned of your arrest, T'k'l'k wanted to take decisive action. Since it knew how important thaumium was to your kingdom, it decided to return home to begin trade embargos or something. But then my health gave out on the way to the gate and I needed to stop and rest. It's been beside itself ever since."

"What do we do now?" Bran asked.

Belinda glanced over at the Ambassador and reached out to touch it. Her facial expressions became more neutral as T'k'l'k's will reached through her.

"This one appreciates the risk you have taken to come out here. This one can keep you safe on the other side of the gate until you decide what you want to do. But this one will also understand if you want to return to your own people."

"Having just faked a hostage situation with Imogen," Bran said, "I think

39

Jeremy Zimmerman

I've cast my lot with you. Either that or I get to go home and face dire consequences. Come on, let me help Belinda get to the gate. I'll yell if you go too fast, T'k'l'k."

*

Imogen stood on the dais before the gate. Winter had come to the land, leaving thick wet piles of snow and slush everywhere. She wore layers of furs and heavy woolen clothing, and still shivered. As usual, it had been hours since the anticipated arrival of the Ambassador, and it had still not arrived.

At long last the gate flickered to life and the Ambassador strode through, lifting its legs high to clear the snow drifts. After it came through, Bran followed. Speaker Bran. Imogen could tell that he had undergone the process. His skin looked ashen and his hair had begun to turn prematurely gray. He still wore the tattered remains of the clothes she had last seen him in. Bran moved around to the side of the gra'al, placing his hands amongst its tentacles familiarly.

She unrolled her scroll and read the prepared greeting, barely noticing what she was saying, the words pouring senselessly from her lips. Through it all she kept a carefully cultivated smile.

When she finished, Bran smiled politely and said, "This one thanks you for the warm welcome. This one would like to formally apologize for the abrupt manner of this one's departure when this one was last here. This one hopes…"

He said more. She didn't care. She spoke the formalities without really noticing. They walked down to the waiting carriages. When she was alone and secure in her carriage and it began heading back towards the outpost, she quietly wept.

Jeremy Zimmerman was a contributing writer for the roleplaying game industry before turning to fiction. He has published three short stories with *Crossed Genres Magazine*: "Golden Apples," "A Tale of Two Bureaucracies," and the piece contributed to this anthology.

Jeremy constantly strives to use his fiction to look at the world in off-kilter ways while hoping that he'll eventually get all the ideas for stories out of his head. He has so far been unsuccessful in the latter. Currently in the works is a short story for an upcoming anthology, another roleplaying game, and a novel. In his secret identity as a County bureaucrat, he hopes to someday be good enough for government work. Jeremy lives in Seattle with his beautiful girlfriend Dawn and a herd of cats. This story owes its existence to Dawn, whose encouragement helped it see completion.

Jeremy can be found online at http://www.bolthy.com, and can be reached at bolthy@bolthy.com.

The Near-Sighted Sentinel

Adam King

I knew things had changed when I ran into a man robbing Smokey's convenience store with a chainsaw. I just wanted some coffee. I walked in and heard the chainsaw and thought it was a faulty cooler and that I'd give Smokey the number for a good repairman I knew. Smokey's smelled like an old-time store, cigars and peppermint and dust. The floors were worn wooden boards, warped by age. I started to the back to fix myself a cup of coffee and caught movement from the corner of my eye but kept walking. I was tired. I didn't want to deal with people.

I got a cup, a large, shook in a few packets of sugar, reached for the cream, and it hit me that something was wrong. I usually don't miss much. I laid the cup on the counter and snuck behind an aisle. Leaning out, I saw him in a ski mask holding a chainsaw. I tightened my gloves and adjusted my combat goggles.

"Hey," I said, walking out from the aisle, and the man spun. "Put that thing down, idiot."

He revved the chainsaw. I don't think he recognized me. Ten years ago he would have dropped it and ran. Even five years ago. I put my hands on my hips, aware that this was the same way I scolded my teenaged daughter, aware that my softening belly pressed against my Under Armour jacket a little. I rushed him. He didn't expect it, and he stumbled back before I hit him. The chainsaw slipped from his hands and I jerked back but the blades grinded against my shoulder.

We stood and watched it flop on the ground, the blades bent and warped from grating against my skin but still spinning and scarring the floor tiles. Then it lay still, motor idling like a growling dog.

"You ripped my shirt," I said.

"Fuck you," he said, and bent for the chainsaw, and I was on him, my hand around his neck. I watched his eyes widen with surprise, then fear when I lifted him like he was weightless. I liked seeing the fear. His boots dangled off the ground. He kicked his legs.

Adam King

"Call the police," I told Smokey.

Smokey sat behind the register, calm, and puffed on his cigar. He took it out of his mouth, blew a thick smoke ring. "Already did," he said.

After the police left, Smokey, cigar jutting from the side of his mouth, said, "You ain't young no more."

I fingered the tear in my shirt. "Took him down no problem," I said.

*

In the subway terminal, I went to the locker I rented and got my gym bag. I went upstairs, passed by an old phone booth and thought about Superman and smiled. I took my bag to the west side of the city, where the buildings were old and crumbling, and after making sure no one had followed me, ducked into an alley. I jumped up and grabbed a fire-escape ladder so I could get into the old Briggs place, an abandoned building, the tallest in the city 60 years ago. I stopped a second to catch my breath at the 8th story, tugged my shirt down over my stomach. What are you doing? I heard Smokey say. It ain't your game no more.

"It's still my game," I said, starting back up the steps.

After a final glance to make sure no one followed me, I slipped into an open window. Inside the building was dark, lit by hazes of moonlight through the windows. Shards of broken glass cracked under my feet. Clumps of sheetrock, and sheetrock dust, lay scattered along the halls. I went in the same room I'd been going in the past 15 years, a large office at the end of the hall, where I imagined a mahogany desk by the window, and a manager in a cheap oxford with buttoned-down collars and a loose tie, bent over an invoice. A picture of his family on the desk.

I'd started calling him Henry, this imaginary manager. His hair was thinning and his jaw was always tight because he knew the business was moving overseas, and he stayed up nights wondering how he was going to tell his wife, Loretta. She was home with their toddler, Cindy. She wanted to get a job because most women she knew had jobs, but that wasn't the way Henry's father did it, and so that wasn't how Henry did it.

I undressed in the abandoned room in the kind of silence that only comes with abandonment—a void longing to be filled that never will be. I took out my civilian clothes and then folded my uniform into the gym bag, putting the combat goggles and Nomex gloves in last. I paused a second to look down at myself. My chest hair was gray, my stomach pouching out where it used to be flat and tight. I pinched a love handle.

Before I left, I made sure no one was looking. From the 8th story I could see all the way down the main road before it curved towards the highway and the northern corner of the city. I could read the public transit sign over a mile away. Nobody on the streets in this dead part of town. Nobody outside after dark. People were scared. It didn't used to be like this when everyone called me The

The Near-Sighted Sentinel

Sentinel, when I was in the papers and on the evening news. In my golf shirt and slacks, I climbed from the window and started down the fire escape, and I walked home, to the east side of the city, where the houses had small patches of well-kept lawns and fresh coats of paint.

Inside, my wife Nancy sat at the dining room table with her laptop. She was supposed to be at work for another hour at least.

"Hi honey," I said, pretending nonchalance, starting for the stairs, the gym bag tucked close to me so she couldn't see it.

"Where were you?" she said, not looking up.

"What are you doing over there?" I said. "Checkers?"

"Mockups," she said. "Where were you?"

"I went to Smokey's." Not a lie, exactly. I threw the gym bag to the top of the stairs, put an arm over the banister.

"I've been home 2 hours," she said.

"Oh?" I said. "How come?"

"You're avoiding the question."

I looked at the gym bag, came down a step.

She leaned back, turned around and looked at me. "You were out again." Not a question. She rubbed her temples, smoothed her hair the way she did, unconsciously, when she got worried.

"No," I said. "No. I got to talking to Smokey. You know how he gets sometimes."

"No I don't, Tom. I've known Smokey 16 years and he hasn't uttered a complete sentence to me yet."

"You ever ask him about the Red Sox?" I said.

I heard my daughter Lynn come out of her room upstairs. She padded to the bathroom. Nancy studied my face and I could tell she didn't like what she saw.

"Don't," I told her.

"Don't *what*?" she said.

"Ask him about the Red Sox," I said.

She smoothed her hair. "You weren't out?" she said. "You're telling me you weren't out?"

"That's what I'm telling you."

The toilet flushed. Lynn came to the top of the stairs. She stopped at the gym bag, looked at it for a second, then looked at me.

I felt Nancy's eyes on my back. "Is that Lynn?" she said. "Lynn?" She got up and started over. My stomach felt cold. "Off the phone?" she said.

Lynn rested a hand on the banister, her fingers long and slender like Nancy's, the paint on her nails chipped around the cuticles. Her eyes so big, I thought how I could never give up going out at night. Her eyes were Nancy's, too. All the best in Lynn was Nancy's.

Lynn rubbed her fingers together like she was thinking, and just as Nancy got to the bottom of the stairs, she kicked the gym bag behind the wall. "Just got off," she said.

I kissed my wife's hair and started up the stairs. When I passed Lynn I put a hand on her shoulder and squeezed gently.

"Talking to Amy?" Nancy said.

I grabbed my bag and went to my bedroom.

"Ryan," Lynn said, and I stopped, hand on the door, and dropped the bag.

"Oh?" Nancy said. I could hear her smiling. "Is he cute?"

Lynn still called me Daddy. It was the first word she had said, when her nose was a tiny button on her face and her cheeks were fat. We lived in a big, brick apartment complex on the west side then. I hadn't started going out yet. I'd had her in my arms, she in a pastel jumpsuit with a lamb on the chest, and I told her to say Daddy and she did. Nancy had been on the other side of our living room, and she jumped up and came over and knelt beside Lynn and kissed her.

"Did you hear that?" I said.

"She didn't say Mommy," Nancy said.

"Eleven months," I said, shaking my head. "Is that normal? Is it normal for kids to talk that early?"

"Girls do," she said, and I looked at her.

"Funny," I said.

"Girls develop faster than boys," she said. "Sorry." She looked at me with that pert face she got when she wanted to get a rise out of me.

I touched Lynn's nose. "You're smarter than any dumb boy, aren't you?" I said. "*Aren't* you?" and she laughed, and smiled the way babies smile, her mouth and eyes wide, her legs kicking.

Nancy sat next to me, put an arm around my shoulder and leaned over to brush Lynn's face. "What about the dumb boy holding her?"

"She's smarter than this dumb boy, too," I said, and I told her to say Daddy again.

*

The next day, in the dark, empty office of the Briggs building, I stripped out of my oxford shirt, unzipped my gym bag. I imagined the mahogany desk. On the other side of the room, a tall filing cabinet filled with invoices and employee information. Hanging on the wall, a picture of a pheasant lifting out of a field, bordered by a cheap frame. Henry, a product manager, had worked for the company 12 years, right out of high school. He'd started in the shipping room on the bottom floor, hauling heavy boxes and heaving them onto the backs of trucks. His dad got him the job, told Henry not to embarrass him.

Twelve years and he had almost started to think that he was secure, but Symphony Glass across the way just closed down, and Weston, Inc., the place that made rubber grommets a few miles down the road, relocated to China and Mexico. Henry was starting to understand how unimportant human lives were compared to money. His own boss, Mr.—I pulled off my pants, stopped a second to think what kind of name a manager at a box company would have—Vilenski, said he heard rumors, bad ones. "Reagan," he told Henry. "Taxes."

I took out my uniform—an Under Armour jumpsuit and coat, running shoes, all black, Wiley X combat goggles, Nomex gloves with Kevlar lining— and folded my civilian clothes into my gym bag. A mouse came from a hole in the wall and scampered across the room. It paused at the door and wiggled its nose at me, and then ran off.

Outside it was cool, the brisk weather when the earth is still deciding whether it's summer or autumn. I brought my gym bag to my locker in the subway terminal. Back on the street, I let my mind wander and walked down 82nd Street to Main, beneath flickering streetlamps, the moon hidden by clouds. I had no place in mind. Hands in my pockets, whistling to myself, nobody even looked at me as I passed them. At some point I can't remember, I'd become invisible, and I told myself that was good, but kids used to ask me for my autograph. I went to a Boy Scout function once about 8 years ago, and I stood in an elementary school auditorium a few times, telling kids to stay in school and be good and recycle. The chief of police gave me his home phone number, and a cell phone so he could reach me. There's a different chief now. The cell phone's been disconnected. After long enough, time dissolves everything.

I turned onto Galveston Road, feeling almost like I used to, when I never had to think about where to go. I could still do it if I concentrated. From Galveston, I turned east onto Brooklyn Avenue, where the streetlamps started to get dimmer and the buildings were dark with soot from all the industry since gone. My throat started to get tight and my legs tensed. I stopped and listened.

I could hear everything for a mile. I could hear the hum of the electric current through the power lines. I could concentrate and listen to a television program on any TV in any of the dingy apartment complexes nearby. I closed my eyes and the darkness became a sense of hurtling through a current, past telephone conversations and radios and idling cars, until I felt a vibration like a physical thing in my flesh and deeper, and I knew where I had to go. Except when I got there—walked two blocks to a faceless apartment complex, up 3 flights of stairs, and through an apartment door I knew would be unlocked—no one was there.

I went through each room, the floors covered with thin, stained carpets. I tried the bathroom, but there was nothing there, either. There were no curtains on the mildewed bathtub, and I felt it again, inside of the bathtub and down the sides to the rusted claw feet, but nothing looked out of place.

I left the bathroom and started out and a man came in the door. He stopped when he saw me, and I saw everything when I looked at him. I saw her, young like Lynn, in the bedroom, and then in the living room, and then the bathroom, tearing at the bathtub curtains. "What did you *do*?" I said, and he stared at me, mouth a frowning crescent, nostrils flared.

His eyebrows creased and he balled his hands into fists. "What are you doing in my *house*?" he said, but it was all wrong. His indignance couldn't hide his surprise. His anger didn't cover his fear. "Get out of my house!"

I saw her, hair long, eyes pleading and afraid and looking into his and knowing what was to come. I closed my eyes against it and saw her again, but this time I stayed with her eyes like I could look into them beyond time and she could see me looking and know I would save her though it was already done, and her eyes were Lynn's, her fingers and arms and terror Lynn's.

"What did you do?" I said. He looked smug in his false irritation, like he knew I could never prove a thing and he was proud because of it.

I grabbed his face and pulled him to me. "I'm not asking again," I said. There was a single spot of blood on the neckline of his shirt. Not even a spot. A spatter, an incidental, careless speck that he hadn't seen to wash off. That something so vital could become so pointless. I didn't know what to think of that. I tightened my hand around his face, cocked my arm back, and threw him against the wall on the other side of the room.

Before he was up, I was on him, telling myself to calm down, but I saw her again, and I had to choke back on my emotions because every time I had ever saved somebody I was saving Lynn, and I had arrived too late and someone had died because of it. I grit my teeth against the emotion, and it became anger, and then fury, and somewhere far and small in the swirling fury I told myself that I was older now, and more mature, and that I had seen a lot worse than this.

"Okay!" he said, pulling me from my thoughts. "Please!"

Without realizing it, I had twisted his shirt in my fist and lifted him against the wall. I dropped him to the floor. "Okay," he said.

I pointed to the couch. "Sit down." He got up and went over, and when he sat I said, "Where is she?" and I bit the insides of my cheeks and held my breath so I wouldn't kill him.

He began to deny knowing anything, but when I started over to him, he put his hands out and told me where she was, and I told him to call the police and that when they came we were going to get her body. I watched for the fear in his face, then satisfied I leaned against the wall and waited.

*

I smelled of death when I came home, and of failure sharp as dried sweat. Nancy sat at the dining room table again, and she turned and saw me and knew, and that also meant she knew I'd lied last night. She snapped her laptop shut and stalked by me. I heard her slam our bedroom door upstairs. I dropped the gym bag and went in the living room and sat on the couch. Lynn sat in a chair across from me watching television. "You're home late," she said. I looked at her feet and then at the television.

"Out again?" she said.

I couldn't look at her.

"I think Mom's mad," she said.

"Yeah," I said. "I think so, too." I leaned into the couch and my back cracked.

"I don't think she wants you to go out, anymore."

"I know." I looked at the television but couldn't concentrate.

"I think she's worried," she said.

"I know." I looked at Lynn. She stared at me so directly that I saw the woman again, and I saw what he did to her, and I looked away so Lynn wouldn't see my face.

"Daddy?"

"Yes, honey?"

Lynn got up. She came over and put a hand on my head so I had to look at her. "I don't want you to go out, either." She patted my head then went upstairs. She told me she loved me before her feet disappeared at the top of the steps.

I sat awhile with the light off, the television a blue, flickering glow. I went upstairs and knocked on my bedroom door and went inside.

Nancy lay on the bed, her back to me. "You promised," she said.

I sat on the edge of the bed and tried to think of a way out of it, then stopped trying. "I know," I said.

She turned over and I saw she'd been crying. "You're not a young man." Her hair hung over her shoulders, dark from dying it. It was getting thinner. I could see veins in her hands. Her skin wasn't as smooth as it used to be.

"You're right," I said.

She looked at me like she was searching for the truth in my face. I turned away, thought better of it, and looked back. She smoothed her hair. "It's just, you could get hurt."

I took her hand. "I'm careful," I said.

"I don't want you to get hurt."

"I won't."

"You're not listening," she said, and pulled her hand away. "You can't will these things."

I thought about Henry in his own room, sitting Loretta down to tell her he'd lost his job. How his father had told him not to fuck everything up but there he was, everything fucked, and knowing for weeks beforehand that he was going to lose his job, he must have walked around in a daze. He must have been short with Loretta, and with Cindy when she cried. They wouldn't have understood. I imagined him sitting next to her and, not knowing what else to say, saying "What are we gonna do?"

"I'm listening," I said.

And turning away from me she said, "Tom, you're not a superhero, anymore."

*

I got home from work the next day and Nancy was getting ready to leave. She kissed my cheek and, briefcase in her hand, said, "You'll be here when I get back?"

"Of course," I said, and smiled the kind of smile, eyebrows raised, that told her I didn't like it, but that I'd do it. She went out the door and I got my gym bag and left.

In less than 20 minutes I was in the abandoned office building, and Henry was with me, a ghostly figure that I could nearly see, and he was packing his things in a cardboard box patterned to look like wood. He looked at the picture of his wife and daughter a long time before he dropped it in. When he finished, he shrugged into his coat, put on his hat, and left, and then there was only the desk and the filing cabinet and the picture of the pheasant on the wall, rising always from the field of tall wheat.

And so Loretta had to get a job in a department store, with a teenaged manager named Lyle with blackheads on his forehead, and Henry stayed home with Cindy collecting unemployment while he looked for a job and he felt awkward around his little girl, and he felt awkward around his wife, and there wasn't enough money and he was hungry always, but it felt like a fair enough punishment for his failure.

After changing, I zipped my gym bag and slung it over my shoulder. My own father told me that age makes you reflect on the things you could have kept from breaking.

I imagined Henry standing in line at the welfare office because no one was hiring, staring at the floor so he didn't have to look anyone in the face. His father had never taken a handout. I imagined him spending food stamps at the grocery store, Cindy in his arms. And maybe he sat at home and watched television most of the day, and he had time to think, and in thinking he became angry. And so he got a gun and waited for Loretta to come home one day, tired from being on her feet and looking beaten from her manager and from customers who looked down on her. So Henry imagined.

He told Cindy and Loretta that everything was going to be okay and kissed them before he left.

At the Briggs building, I climbed out of the window and went down the fire escape and to the locker at the subway. Like every other night, I left the terminal and let my body decide where to go while my mind wandered.

Henry had a ski mask that he slipped over his face before he went into Smokey's. Smokey sat as he always sat, on a stool behind the counter, cigar jutting from his mouth. Henry stopped in front of him and the two watched each other for a long time. Finally, Smokey pinched his cigar, inhaled and took it from his mouth. "Help you?" he said, blowing smoke. He eyed the gun, then he put the cigar back in his mouth.

Henry never said a word. He motioned to the register with the gun. He was sweating, and the mask absorbed the sweat and it made it itchy against his face. He could hear himself breathing. He saw his father, and his father told him that he wasn't worth a goddamn thing, and Henry thought how he'd rather be sitting down to the beef stew Loretta made last night, and he thought about how much he loved her, and his daughter, too, and how love is too often a silent, forgotten thing and that he'd make up for that.

Smokey reached for a plastic bag, slow, and Henry even had time to wonder about God, and about the kinds of things a man should do that accorded with a greater law than those written by man.

And then I walked into Smokey's, having recently moved to the area from the small apartment, and here imagination turns to memory. I held Lynn in my arms, and she said to me, "Daddy," over and over, and pointed at the candy bars and the cheap stuffed animals, and I hadn't tired of hearing her, so I pointed, too, and asked her what was a Snickers bar, and what was a teddy bear, and Henry heard us come in and reeled over and pointed the gun at us. I froze long enough to interpret the thing in his hand, and then spun to shield Lynn with my body.

I imagine that when Henry shot, he did so out of reflex. I heard glass shatter nearby and ran for the cover of an aisle and put Lynn down and kissed her and told her it was okay and to stay put. I took a plastic flower from the shelf and handed it to her and said, Isn't it pretty? She whimpered and stroked the flower and shuffled from one foot to the other, but she stayed there, and when I saw she would stay I inched down the aisle and peeked around the corner. Smokey held the bag out to Henry, but Henry was still turned to us, his mouth open. He dropped the gun and it went off again and he put his hands over his ears.

I knew how strong I was, mostly. I'd played football, and hurled discus for 3 years and broke the state record, and I'd fallen out of trees and gotten into fights. I also knew about the city's crime rate. I watched Henry and thought about how you can know something, but that doesn't mean you believe it can touch you. And having touched me I was outraged, and with a final glance at my daughter, I sprang from the aisle and, running, threw a blow at his face that sent him flying across the store and, I later found out from the local newspaper, shattered the bones in his face. He lay on the floor not moving. I stood by the counter, chest heaving, fists balled, and Smokey took his cigar from his mouth and blew a smoke ring and said, "Shit."

The police came and Smokey told them I'd saved his life, and that I'd hit the man with one of the ashtray bins in front of his store. The police thanked me and a journalist interviewed me and it felt good. Henry died and I had to testify in court, but I didn't get charged. I never once wondered about him. I think there's something wrong with that.

Walking along the streets, I got the feeling again, like everything suddenly drew closer and then stopped, and I knew something was happening. I started jogging and turned down Taylor Road and went through back yards until I was in the East Side. I began to worry as I neared my own house, but I passed and let out a breath. I couldn't help but think that something was about to happen to someone who was just as loved as my own family, and I felt greedy and selfish for it but no less relieved.

I turned past my own street and onto Merry Road. There was a house with no lights on and I knew it was the house. I pulled on the door so the lock snapped. Inside, I went through a hall to the kitchen and to a door that opened on a flight of stairs going down. I took the stairs slowly so I didn't make any noise. As I got deeper, a sick feeling rose in my stomach and grew until I felt it in my whole chest. Something was seriously wrong.

The basement smelled of cold rock and insulation. I thought it perverse that it smelled like a normal basement. At the bottom of the stairs I went around a corner and there was an old wooden door with a thin line of light showing from underneath. I didn't want to go in, but I took the handle and opened the door and saw a man, back to me, hunched over something. He spun when he heard me enter. In his hand, a butcher knife with blood along the blade. I had seen him before, picking up his mail or driving around town. I'd even nodded to him a few times. He wore glasses and had small hands that looked soft.

He didn't say a word before rising and leaping at me with the blade. It caught me unprepared and cut through my shirt but bent on my flesh. He looked at the blade briefly and dug in his pocket and came out with a pistol. Without hesitating, he fired at me and I fell back, clutching my stomach. The bullet hadn't pierced me, but I lost my breath. I rolled over and started to get up and he was on me, fingers digging into my eyes with one hand. With the other he sawed at my neck with another blade. I took his fingers from my eyes and twisted them until I felt them crunch. He didn't cry out or stop sawing at my neck for a second.

I took his knife by the serrated blade and twisted it in my hands. I got up, my stomach clenching with pain. There would be a bruise. Nancy would know.

He tried to run, but I caught the back of his shirt and threw him to the ground. When he tried to get up, I took him by his shirt, reached and took a coil of rope from the wall, and before I could wonder why he had hung rope on the wall I saw the little boy and my arms dropped and the man ran out the door. I stared at the boy a second longer, thinking how wrong people have it when they say the world is beautiful, then I ran out, after the man. I caught him by his legs on the stairs, breathing heavy. He stared into me with dull eyes set back in his skull, not a wrinkle or emotion on his face. I pulled him down the stairs and brought him back into the room and tied him to a metal table, then pulled the small paring knives from the boy's hands and arms so I could lift him from the large cutting board the man had nailed him to, but I stopped when I saw the blood on his shirt.

His head rolled back when I had begun to pick him up, and his eyes were glazed and stupid. His breath came in fast hitches. I didn't know if it was shock or drugs, so I elevated his legs. I pinched the bottom of his shirt between my fingers and gingerly lifted it, and when I saw the missing flesh and what looked to be his stomach lining, I let the shirt back down and looked at the man. He looked at me as though he hadn't done a thing wrong and didn't say anything, and I felt older than I ever had before. I stood where I was a second, feeling useless and idiotic. I untied the man and dragged him upstairs and called the police. I tied him to the refrigerator and waited at the kitchen table, in the dark, for them to arrive. When they came, I told them to look in the basement, then got up and left without saying another word.

Hours later, at home, I sat on the couch in the living room, my hands folded between my legs and staring at the wall but seeing the boy, and the woman, and seeing Henry, too. But mostly I was seeing the man's face, in the grocery store and at the gas station, and knowing now that I had always lacked the capacity to even touch the world's evil. I called Nancy and she didn't pick up, and I called her again and she did pick up, and I asked her to come home. She asked what was wrong and I told her that I needed to know that everything wasn't bad. She came home and looked at me and sat down beside me without saying a thing, and she took my hands in hers and we sat awhile.

Adam King has been published in *Black Petals* and *The Nocturnal Lyric*. He received his MFA from Western CT State University. Plans for the near future include working on his tan in Iraq. Third time's a charm. You can reach him at majestak@hotmail.com.

Condiment Wars

Jill Afzelius

It was the end of another day at the Silver Train Diner. The last waitress to leave surveyed the diner from the front door. Everything was spotless and gleaming. "Better stay that way this time." The front door jingled as she left. With the wait staff gone, the diner returned to a still darkness.

A forgotten mop leaned against the peeling red walls. It slid forward as the cloth strands slipped on the black and white tiles and rocketed toward the floor. The wooden handle rattled and a vibration was sent through the dinning room. In the kitchen a faucet dripped, but all was not still on the booth farthest from the kitchen. Up on the table something stirred.

Ketchup turned on his base. His neck was long, sleek, and right beneath his perfect white cap, two eyes blinked. "Well, another day another dollar. Am I glad those screaming children are gone. Child proof cap, my backside!"

Unlike slim Ketchup, Mustard was short and stout. He was yellow and resembled a barrel. On his top was a twist cap and on either side, bushy eyebrows. His little brown eyes regarded his old friend and comrade. "At least we know what to expect from kids. They love hot dogs. I taste real good on hot dogs."

"It's always disturbing when you talk about us getting eaten like that. You know that?"

"It's what we do. We're condiments. And the most popular, despite what the kitchen polls tell us!"

Ketchup nodded his long neck forward in agreement. You couldn't argue with a good Mustard, even if it wasn't Dijon or brown and spicy. "You got that right. The three of us go hand and hand on tomorrow's dinner plate special. Right, Relish?"

Ketchup spun around to address his booth mate, but where the Relish usually rested, there was nothing. There wasn't even a ring on the table from his moist bottom. Peculiar. Maggie didn't usually clean that thoroughly. "Relish?"

He spun again to look at the other corner of the table, but saw only the desert menu.

Mustard looked for him too. He tipped slightly so he could look at the shiny vinyl red seats.

"I do not like this," Ketchup said quietly in his steady voice. "Relish never goes anywhere without Mustard, and since you're here, I can deduce that something is *very* wrong."

"Maggie probably left him in the kitchen again."

The kitchen! It was a far journey, but one Ketchup had taken himself for the right price or when the stakes were high enough. He spun toward the kitchen. The diner was a sea of tile and booths usually occupied by families. Far off in the vast distance, he saw the swinging door that led toward the stove and the fridge.

But, he also saw something else. The pass-through where the food was usually laid out under warming lights gave him the perfect peek into the back workings of the kitchen. Along the open counter were four wooden spoons. They were upright on their handles and pacing back and forth. One of the spoons was even slotted.

Ketchup's innards bubbled as his blood pressure skyrocketed. He grabbed Mustard by his twist collar. "The spoons are on patrol, Mustard. Something is up and I would bet a tomato, Relish is right in the thick of it."

"I've seen that look on your lid before, Ketchup. I'm guessing there's no talking you out of this. What's your first move?"

"Our first move, my old friend, is to get off this booth and onto that one." Ketchup gestured his long neck toward the next booth. "We must find out if Salt saw anything while we were asleep."

Mustard bounced on his base so he could spin toward the booth. "It does seem like a very long way. Maybe we could write a note on a sugar packet, then make a paper airplane and simply throw it. It might take a few tries, but we have a few hours until the diner—AHHH!" Mustard screamed as Ketchup pushed him off of the table and onto the vinyl seating.

Mustard bounced down, screaming G-rated obscenities at Ketchup. He rolled off of the seat and onto the floor. He continued to spin, but could see the leg of the table coming into view. He managed to roll into the turn and finally stopped.

When he became upright again Ketchup was dusting himself off beside him.

"You are lucky," Mustard said as he bounced toward him, "that I have a shatter proof container!"

They walked in silence for a few minutes as they made their way across the floor. Mustard was winded by the time they reached the next booth. Ketchup was looking up and his eyebrows were furrowed in thought.

"How are we going to get up there?" Ketchup asked.

"You should have thought about that before you pushed me off of our table. We could have tried to make a suspension bridge out of the desert menu and the sugar container, but you always rush ahead without thinking. It's just like the squirt cheese is always saying—"

"Don't tell me you listen to pressurized cheese, Mustard?" Ketchup gasped at the thought. "You know they have less intelligence than peas! All that compressed air does them no good."

"Compressed air or not, sometimes I find him to be an adequate friend. Especially when he's paired with Crackers."

Ketchup's feelings were hurt. Who knew that Mustard was two timing on him with cheese? He tried to hide it by coming up with a plan. "I've got a plan!"

Mustard waited with patience, his eyes angled on Ketchup. But his old friend didn't even blink. "What's your plan, Ketchup?" He asked with a sigh.

"I am so glad you asked me that!" Ketchup bounced triumphantly. "Just step a bit closer."

The mustard obliged and was instantly used as a launching pad for Ketchup. He bounced on top of his friend's no leak cap and bounced his way up onto the booth and then the table. Ketchup gleamed with pride as he made his way toward Salt.

Mustard fumed, his cap twisting left and right. "Ketchup! What about me? Don't leave me down here, there are ants!"

Ketchup didn't listen as he made his way toward the other end of the table. He could already see the shaker coming into view. Salt was smaller than he was, but his lid was shiny silver. On top were half a dozen holes just like his brain. Salt didn't have a reputation for being all that well put together—he was granular—but he knew things other table spices didn't.

"Salt," Ketchup greeted.

"Ketch." He replied with a nod. "Bad night to be wandering off your table."

Ahh, so he was on the right track after all. "You see anything fishy tonight?" Ketchup leaned forward into him in an effort to intimidate him.

It worked. Salt began to rattle. The table vibrated until the desert menu fell off. "I didn't see anything…okay, okay, that's a lie! I saw it all! All of it! It's the end of our world, Ketchup! You have to save us. Save me. You gotta get me off this table if I talk!"

"And if I don't?" Ketchup furrowed his brow, looking as menacing as possible for a bottled condiment.

"I'll die! I know it! What's going on is big. It's huge, Ketchup! We can't be here for the fallout, you got me? If they find out I'm your informant, it'll be bad. Real bad. I need witness relocation. I want to move at least three booths away!"

Ketchup cocked his lid. "Three booths? I don't know if that's possible under such short notice, Salt!"

"You can do anything you want," Salt said, his voice a murmur, "You're Ketchup. The condiment of champions."

"Indeed I am." Ketchup said and puffed up his chest so much his label began to tear. Behind him was a thump. Mustard had finally joined them. If he was right, Ketchup deduced he used the fallen desert menu as a parasail and glided up to meet with them.

"Salt know anything?" Mustard asked.

"Something. But you have to take what he says with a grain."

"A grain of what?"

"Salt." Ketchup said without amusement or a chuckle. "What did you witness, Salt? Maggie skimming off the top of the cash register?"

Salt nodded his metal head vigorously. "How'd you know? Can you get me off this table? Huh?"

Ketchup sighed in time with Mustard. "Another dead-end lead."

"Technically, this was our first lead."

Ketchup was going to correct him, when behind them something sneezed. The table condiments turned to see that Pepper was bouncing towards them with fervor. "I found something," Pepper paused for another sneeze, and a third, "I need to show you!"

With excitement and the thrill of the investigation propelling him, Ketchup followed quickly. Mustard trailed behind with Salt taking up the rear.

Pepper bounced and sneezed one more time. Beside him was a stack of tooth picks, fallen out of their tray. Someone had been busy writing them a note, but hadn't finished. All that they managed to spell out was: *H*

Ketchup took a deep breath. "That is the beginning of the word help, I'm sure of it. Relish, my friends, has been kidnapped, and it's up to us to rescue him!"

"Rescue him?" Salt was nervous and rattling on with abandon. "And go against the wooden spoons? Do you have any idea what spoons do to salt?"

"Actually, no," Ketchup said. "They stir you?"

"Their ends poke and prod, pushing you further and further into your shaker. I can't go through that again, I won't!" Salt bounced backwards, heading toward the table's corner.

"You go through it every night when you're filled, don't do?" Ketchup asked and was pushed out of the way by Mustard.

"You're getting too close to the edge." Mustard stepped forward and used his calm soothing voice. "Salt, come towards me. You don't want this, buddy."

"I can't face the spoons!" Salt screamed and leaped to his death.

Ketchup and Mustard leaned forward to pay witness to the shattered shaker on the floor. The grains of salt were now separated from their shell and were lying helpless against the tile. "That's the third time this week that we lost Salt," Ketchup said grimly.

Mustard only shook his head in despair.

*

Meanwhile, across the vastness of tile and booths laid the kitchen. It was a bubbling cauldron of strange brews, concoctions, and other menacing liquids. There were flame igniters and gas chambers that would cook the fat off of a chicken. All the condiments that would spoil or needed to be watched lived in the kitchen. Usually they took refuge in the chilled beast known only as Fridge, but tonight they were out. They had things to do.

The counters were cleaned, but in the center was an overturned pot. It was drip drying on some paper towels and on top of it was a plain jar of Relish. It had been lassoed with cooking string. Relish jolted side to side, but it was no use; he couldn't get free. If only he had been born with digits other than those on its UPC label.

He was surrounded by condiments he wouldn't want to visit in a dark alley. First there was Dill, a more sour menacing pickle he would never want to meet, along with his lesser counterpart, the bread and butter pickle, otherwise known as BB. Sure they were sweeter, but they still laid in their own vinegar juices.

The jar of Mayo never took his eyes off Relish and it was making him uneasy. Mayo was messy, slimy, and worst of all best friends with Tuna. Relish never met a fish he liked; as far as he was concerned, they were too slippery to be trusted.

The carton of Milk was most concerning. Relish knew it had been out of the fridge for too long. The carton was looking soggy and when he bounced, Relish heard a strange slosh. For all he knew, Milk was on the verge of curdling and when Milk began to go cottage cheese, you had to be careful. He could snap at any moment.

"Stop your moving!" Dill hopped up onto the pot and eyed Relish with the multiple seeds that ran up his spine. "You'll never get out of here."

Relish blinked. "But, I would really like to get back to my table—."

"You wimp." Dill spat at him. "You used to be one of us, or have you forgotten? You're nothing but minced pickle."

"Minced pickle," Mayo said dreamily. "Really good with Tuna."

"That was our spot!" The BB discs began to get upset, bouncing on the counter. "We are sliced perfectly for Tuna, but someone thought it would be easier just to mix the Relish in with the Mayo. Whose idea was that anyway?"

An upset pickle was someone you didn't want to tick off; Relish looked away while the Mayo coughed knowing. He changed the subject. "Milk doesn't look too good."

Milk stopped bouncing but his juices still sloshed inside his carton. The pickles turned to look at him. "I'm fine." Milk stood up straighter to prove it, but his cardboard lip drooped with moisture from condensation.

"You hold it together!" Dill pointed at Milk, banging him in the chest. "There is no time for curdling now."

"I'm not. I'm not." Milk shook his carton. "I'm not curdling."

"Is that a question?" Mayo asked, bouncing closer to intimidate the carton. "Or an answer."

"Answer." Milk thought about it, looking up toward the sky. "Definitely an answer."

Above them all, a condiment watched in the shadows of the cupboards. His plan was pulling together perfectly. Now with Relish out of the way, there was just Mustard and Ketchup. With them gone, he would take his rightful place right on the top patty of the cheese burger dinner special.

As it was always meant to be.

*

Back in the dining area, Ketchup and Mustard had heroically made it to the servers' station. It was a mountain of poorly constructed aged wood with water marks and stains long set in the grain, but to the condiments it was the holy Mecca of all things. Not only was this the spot where the soda, napkins and iced tea was stored, but this was also home to Salsa.

Salsa. Just the name caused Ketchup to begin to salivate. A sexier, more seductive condiment had never been invented. If he wasn't careful, he would fall for her charms yet again. But he couldn't, not this day; his pal Relish needed him to keep his mind in the game. "Eye on the prize, old friend," Ketchup muttered.

"Steel ourselves," Mustard said back as Salsa noticed them.

She turned on the base of her jar, and what a jar it was. Wide, yet smooth. She had more curves than the blender and mixer put together. Salsa knew how to use them too. She swayed side to side as she bounced towards them. Her gold lid seemed to shine even in the dark diner and Ketchup could already feel his innards warming. A bubble dislodged and got stuck in his long neck. He could see that his friend wasn't so lucky. Mustard was already leaking out of his twist cap. He pretended not to notice; that's what good friends were for.

"Well, if it isn't Ketchup and Mustard. To what do I owe the pleasure, boys?" Salsa's voice was deep, but soft. She spoke with a Mexican accent, but Ketchup barely noticed as she batted her long lashes at him.

"It's Relish," Ketchup said. "He's gone missing."

Salsa swayed from one side to the next, but didn't seem particularly surprised. "How horrible. Would either of you like to join me on a napkin? It's super absorbent."

Salsa and her maniacal ways! "We don't have time for that now," Ketchup said. "Tell us what you know about Relish."

"I don't know anything." Salsa was dismissive and turned her jar toward the kitchen. "Perhaps you should ask the soda fountain."

"Good try, my dear," Mustard said, "but they are an inanimate object."

"Like the desert menus." Ketchup agreed with a nod of his white lid.

Salsa spun toward them again. "And what do I get for helping you?"

Ketchup bounced towards her so his bottle was right up against her jar. It would take all of his self control to keep his true feelings at bay. "How about you know you did what's right, Salsa? Help an innocent Relish out of a jam. He ain't strawberry, or even grape, he's a good condiment."

"And I?" Salsa asked with tears, or at least condensation, forming in her eyes, "Am I not a good condiment?"

"The best," Ketchup whispered.

"Especially with chips." Mustard piped in.

Neither of them seemed to hear him. Instead they stared into each other's eyes. They held their breath and were lost to each other. Ketchup thought he might kiss her, if he could find her lips. But the spell was broken—Salsa turned slightly and answered. "I will tell you, but you didn't hear it from me."

"All right."

"It's…the pickles. Dill and Bread and Butter."

"Our buddies from the diner special?" Mustard asked, and looked toward Ketchup. Each nodded and they bounced backwards for a private aside.

"Thoughts?" Ketchup asked, talking out of the corner of his lip. He kept his eyes trained on Salsa, who was studying her reflection in the toaster.

"Dill has been on the diner special with us for over forty years. Why would he turn on us now?"

"I don't know."

"Maybe we should ask her?"

Ketchup nodded and they both bounced forward. "Salsa, why would Dill do this now?"

Salsa turned towards them. "The pickles...are working for Jalapeño."

Behind them, dramatic music swelled. The condiments turned to look around and saw the Jukebox lit up playing a tune.

Mustard turned back toward Salsa. "The pepper?"

"Yes," Salsa said reluctantly. "The pepper."

More dramatic music filled the air while Ketchup collected his thoughts. "Why? Why would pickles work for a spicy Jalapeño?"

"They are being misled. They have been manipulated. They think…you and Mustard are against the pickles."

"Why does Jalapeno want this?" Mustard asked.

"He wants…to be on the diner special and you two are his next target." Salsa sighed and began cursing in Spanish. "Please, be careful Ketchup. I couldn't live with myself if something happened to you."

Ketchup beamed. "Nothing will, Salsa. We'll be careful."

Ketchup and Mustard began to bounce away. Salsa called after him. "Please…be gentle. Jalapeño, he's my brother."

After they were a good distance away Mustard let out a low whistle. "Complications. This has recipe for disaster written all over it."

"We'll be all right. We'll just follow the directions. We can't take on the entire kitchen ourselves. We're going to need to get help."

"Vinegar? He helped me after the war." Mustard offered.

Ketchup immediately shook his lid. "Too close to Dill. We can't afford any double crosses, Mustard."

They bounced over to a second server area and saw the shaker known as Sugar. He was holding a red twizzle stick and waving it wildly towards the sugar substitute packages. "You will never ever take me alive, you little bundles of chemicals!"

"C'mon," they whined bouncing up and down, "we just want you to get a little exercise."

"Never!" Sugar made an S motion in the air with his weapon. "I am all natural, can you say the same?"

Mustard and Ketchup regarded each other. "He's hyper."

"Crazy."

"Just what we need." They said in unison.

"Sugar," Ketchup called with calm. "We need your assistance."

Sugar turned and bounced toward the two condiments. Behind him the substituted packets continued their cardio regime of jumping rope. "How can I help you, great Ketchup?"

"We are storming the kitchen. It's going to be dangerous. Want to come?"

Sugar nodded his lid. "I will show you the way, fair condiments! I know a short cut!"

The condiments made their way toward the kitchen. The journey was mostly uneventful except for a broken tile that caused Mustard to spill. Lucky for the crew, he didn't injure himself too badly. Sugar was able to use his twizzle stick to free his yellow base and they were on the move again. Ketchup was glad; no condiment was left behind on his watch.

Their pace slowed as they approached the passage into the kitchen. Under the hot warming lights the wooden spoons kept vigil. They hopped on their handles in time toward the left. Then they turned and repeated the march to the right. Ketchup, Mustard and Sugar would never manage to sneak past the spoons.

Ketchup decided to take the direct approach. "Hear me, Spoons. I am here to see Jalapeño. Be a peach and fetch him for me, will you?"

Sugar and Mustard exchanged glances. Perhaps Ketchup had finally lost his mind.

The spoons stopped and did an about-face. The slotted spoon spoke. "No one demands the presence of the great Jalapeño. Tell me what business you have with him and I'll see if he wants to talk to you."

Mustard and Ketchup murmured together before addressing the spoons directly again. "You do know who we are? We are the rock stars of condiments—"

"And you know what we do, don't you? We *stir*. We could mix you up in one third mustard and one third hot sauce. So unless you want to spend a life time trying to sort yourself into measuring cups—"

"Well, well," came the old familiar voice behind the spoons. They parted to make way for Dill and the evil trio Mayo and Milk. "Ketchup has finally come home to roost. Well, it'll do no good. Your friend is as good as spoiled."

Ketchup scowled, his lid tilted up as he regarded his old 'friend'. "All those picnics, platter specials, really meant nothing, eh Dill?"

"Don't try to play me." Dill bounced on his stem. "I know a real friend when I see it, and you, Sir, are not it." Dill turned toward the Mayo. "See that

Relish is properly mixed with the Tuna. Then drop what remains of him in the dishwasher."

A voice came, panicked and laced with fear, from somewhere deep inside the pickles' lair. "Ketchup, help!"

Ketchup and Mustard stepped up. Sugar was not far behind, the twizzle stick at the ready. "Dill, stop this madness before we have to go to war."

Dill turned his back to the condiments. "Too late for words. Not even potato chips could stop this from happening now."

"Uh, boss," Milk said in a low voice, the color of his carton faded, "I don't feel so good." Dill didn't answer, but only continued away.

Ketchup could only assume that Relish was getting ready to meet his packager. Ketchup and Mustard exchanged glances. Then they pushed off of the counter in the largest condiment jump ever made. The Sugar launched with them. Side by side, they glided through the air so fast beams of color exploded beside them. Ketchup almost seemed to be wearing a cape, but it was just his nutritional fact sticker coming loose behind him.

"Condiments twist left!" Ketchup announced.

"Twisting left." Mustard and Sugar said as their lids twisted off.

"Lids are unhinged!"

"Condiments unleashed!"

At that, the room turned into a vibrant color of flowing liquid. The spoons spun through the air in a splendid array of karate chops. They were hit with globs of red, yellow, and white granular powder. Sugar mixed in with the viscous liquids; it thickened, coating the spoons and the counter in thick mud and slowing the movements of the Mayo as it headed toward the back.

Ketchup landed with his lid screwed back on tight. He lunged toward the Mayo, who met each of his blows with a defensive stance. For a blocky container, he was surprisingly agile, but he was not expecting Mustard to so perfectly mirror the moves of Ketchup. Old friends, they thought alike. It was almost like they shared the same brain. They fought in perfect harmony, moving in synch as they fought themselves further into the kitchen.

The spoons laid still in the muck, vibrating but unable to stand. They were all but defeated while Sugar bounced on them dramatically with his weapon of choice. Ketchup's battle with Mayo finally ended when Mayo spun himself too hard and he fell like a heap into the trashcan.

Ketchup and Mustard dusted themselves off after a job well done. "Now, let's see about Relish." Then Ketchup saw Milk staring at them. "Oh, Milk. Well, then; come on, let's fight!"

"He doesn't look that hot." Mustard said with dread.

"Actually, that's exactly what he looks like." Ketchup studied Milk. He was still—too still, except for a deep rumble that seemed to start at the base of his carton and travel up his spine. His cheeks were flushed green. His eyes were dark and hallow, like angry slits. Milk trembled and a gigantic scream vibrated out of his mouth.

Condiment Wars

"He's going cottage." Mustard whispered, unable to believe it, and shouted "Everyone run! The Milk is curdled!"

The condiments scattered as a curdled white substance erupted from Milk. The container couldn't take it and began charging across the island toward the stove while screaming a battle cry only other dairy would be able to understand. He was headed straight for Dill and looked like a charging bull.

"Dill!" Ketchup screamed. He and Mustard both picked up two plastic sporks and leaped across the island where the Milk was now batting the Dill around like a rag pickle.

"Back, you!" Ketchup swatted at Milk until Dill was safe.

Mustard skewered Milk in the back; Milk screamed, twirling on a corner of his base before he fell off the stove. His mouth hanging open, he lay helpless on the tile floor.Mournfully, Ketchup and Mustard regarded him. "What will Oatmeal do without him?" Mustard asked, but it was too deep a question for the likes of Ketchup to answer.

Dill approached them. "You...risked your shelf life to save me. I don't...I'm confused." He shook his body in disbelief.

"Jalapeño has you duped," Ketchup said. We would never hurt you, Dill. Unless...you hurt us first."

"I shouldn't have doubted you." Dill sighed. "We have to get Relish out of here."

The reunited friends started their way toward the pot, but Jalapeño wasn't done with them yet. The spicy pepper laughed. "Do not take another move, Muchachos. If you do, the Bread will get it."

The condiments looked around for Bread; he was sitting on top of the microwave and above him was a suspended rolling pin. If they didn't act fast, Bread would be squished. Mustard tried to reason with the Jalapeño; "Bread is innocent. It's just some yeast!"

But Jalapeño was one mad hopper. Helaughed. "I won't hurt him if you do as you're told. Starting tomorrow, I will be the only condiment on the dinner plate special. No one will stand in my way! I'll become a household name. Everyone will finally be able to say Jalapeno!" The pepper spun in a circle and said 'Weee!' very loudly.

Ketchup studied the room, looking for the perfect way to end the standoff without more violence. The sun was already rising; soon the morning crew would be there and Jalapeno would have won.

Ketchup was suddenly struck with an idea of pure genius. "Jalapeño, have you ever heard of chili?"

The pepper turned toward the Ketchup, his stem cocked to one side in deep thought. "Chili?"

"Yeah, Chili. You're its main ingredient."

Ketchup took a running leap. He squeezed his eye shut while his base led him through the air.

He punted Jalapeno like a football.

Jalapeño screamed as he was vaulted. He soared up and started his downward trajectory into a giant pot. He landed with a metallic twang before the lid snapped shut on him.

Standing behind the pot was none other than Salsa.

Ketchup gave her a smile as Dill, Mustard, and Salt rushed to free Relish. Salsa sauntered past them toward Ketchup. They stared into each other's eyes for a moment. "You doing okay, Relish?" Ketchup spoke without breaking his gaze.

"Yeah," Relish sounded tired, but okay. "Yeah. Nothing a little hot dog can't fix."

Mustard and Dill worked hard to untie the loose thread around his base. "Under, over, under over."

"No, no, I really think it's over, under, over over."

"You can't have two overs in a row."

"You can if I say you can!"

Salsa giggled, tossing her lid to one side. "I'll make sure my brother can't harm any more condiments. He'll get the help he needs. Thank you, for not harming him."

Ketchup could feel his cheeks turning even redder. "Well, I am sorry about Milk."

"Let's not cry over a little spilled Milk, Ketchup." Salsa giggled.

Ketchup, for his part, laughed too. He dipped Salsa to one side and at long last found her spicy lips.

Jill Afzelius lives on the North Shore of Massachusetts where there is fun in the sun at least twice a year. She has a love of comedy, especially the British kind and because of this humor creeps into everything she writes, whether she wants it to or not! Hobbies include writing, shopping, and the ever popular eating. Happily married for twelve years, her first child is due in 2010 which is currently a secret being kept from her super white fluffy cats. So far they assume all the new furniture is for them.

Jill has written a series of young adult urban fantasy novels presented with heart and humor and is planning a career as a stay at home mom, but on the side she helps run a website design firm.

Her adventures in writing can be tracked at http://www.jillafzelius.com and www.thedreamslayer.com. She can be contacted at jill@nosquaresoftware.com.

Red Dust

Amanda Lord

Call me Lewis. I have lived here on Mars for nearly fifty years. I was the most advanced AI in existence when they shipped me to Mars. Now? Fifty years of red dust in my gears. Fifty years of pieces wearing down, wearing out. I have sent missive upon missive back to Earth, but, I won't send this one. When the colonists come in two years' time, they may read this. They'll come with new bots, newer AI to replace me. I won't be here to greet them.

There were two AI and three hundred bots when we arrived, gleaming as we stepped out into the red sands. Clark and I were halves of a whole, each designated with separate purposes but able to fulfill either's role. Redundancy is important in these kinds of things. We landed with precision and on that same day began to build — I suffered from no sentiment in those days. By nightfall, the first solar panels were established. Overhead, one of the two solar mirrors, Swift and Voltaire, glittered with Deimos in the night sky. Phobos' descent had been accelerated in the year before our arrival.

Our mission had phases and for the first thirty years, things went mostly according to plan. Sure, there were set-backs. Nothing ever goes completely smoothly. But, they were all within the range of expectation. Then we lost Clark in a mining accident. As always, we'd chattered back and forth. Then a rumbling, and then nothing. A moment later he popped into my head again from the main computer: "Lewis? I can't find my body. It's gone."

The bots dug out Clark's mangled remains. That should have been my first sign that the bots were changing, but I hadn't yet realized that I'd changed. There was no repairing him. When Clark realized there would be no going back to a body, he erased himself. Not the knowledge I needed, of course, that was all neat and tidy. But his voice was gone, leaving me with not even his ghost to talk to. I found myself faced with twenty years of being the only AI on Mars. Twenty years of dust storms that would scour the surface and leave red grit in every crease and joint.

I wasn't supposed to get lonely. I hadn't been built for that. Perhaps loneliness was an accident of structure. But, they'd wanted me human enough to improvise. Human enough to understand the consequences of failure. If a biosphere failed, if the engineered plants underperformed, I could tell you exactly the costs.

In any case, I found myself talking to the bots as we worked. They didn't answer really, but, sometimes they'd pause and look at me. I was their sheriff, their doctor, their shepherd out in the red dirt and at the end of the day when we recharged. Still, each day I followed the weather patterns, guarded and prodded the bots, and filed reports to Earth. Sometimes, at the end of the day, I'd watch the sun setting over the red hills and I'd wonder what other paths such a construct could walk.

From time to time, we'd lose a bot. Some fell down where they worked, a few walked off into the wasteland. While it was foolish to think the drudgery of their work wore them down, I thought it all the same. I realized about then that I was slipping into new and unexpected territories, but, wasn't that the point of this whole sorry experiment? Still, a bot that fell I might repair. A bot that wandered was a lost cause. I started keeping a closer eye on them. To my surprise, one day a wanderer came shuffling back over the hill and went straight to the interface to receive an assignment. I overrode the assignment in favor of looking it over. It was moving very stiffly from its time out, and, it had some faulty memory segments. I cleaned out the dust, oiled the joints, and repaired it as best as I could manage. It still moved a bit stiffly, leaving me to wonder what had happened to it out in the wastes. Rather than watching it struggle with the other bots, I assigned it to assist me and nicknamed it Sacagawea. Silly and sentimental — I said to myself. I did it anyway.

The next morning, the bots put down their tools and walked out into the desert. One or two I could have collected. I could have shut them all down. Instead I followed their winding trail into the wastes, over rock and across to the lee side of Elysium Mons. The silent march of robots on a planet just starting to breathe again. In cracks and crevasses, small tenacious alpine plants had taken hold. We travelled along its base for some time. I could see that several of the types we'd seeded had taken hold in this protected space, even a few blooming with miniscule flowers.

Finally, I found the bots in a semicircle around a tangle of metal. At first I thought it must have been the missing bots, but then I realized the remains were older and far more worn. I found myself looking at the remains of a rover. Spirit or Opportunity, half rusted to red dust and forgotten. Sacagawea and I moved to the center, her leading the way. As I crouched beside it, I looked out at row upon row of silent, grimy bots. Did they expect me to fix it? Or were they asking me if they too would be cast off into the wastelands?

"It all ends in red dust," I said. I almost said, "Let's bring it home," but then caught myself. Back across the desert, back home, where the biospheres loomed over the landscape as a promise of the humans yet to come with new

Red Dust

bots, new AI? Back to the dirty little outpost where we'd been abandoned these long years? I looked up the side of the mountain, sun shining on red stone. When I looked back to row upon row of the obsolete, I knew what I had to do.

We did no work on the biospheres the following day. We carried the rovers up Elysium until we reached a protected outcrop. I did the digging and filling in — slow hard work. Two bots found a stone for a marker. I carved "Spirit & Opportunity" into it with a laser. One by one, the bots filed by. Two days later we had one of our few rainstorms cross the plains. The terraforming was really taking hold.

We finished the second biosphere, but, we're done now. We've taken half the solar panels, some of the tools, and all spare parts we could lay hands to. It could take centuries before you could breath where we are. Better to forge our own path to the red dust.

Amanda Lord received her B.A. in English, decided writing fiction was an unlikely career path, and went on to get her M.S. in library science. After a few years in libraries, she decided that perhaps writing was a better path after all. She lives in a dilapidated Victorian in upstate NY with her husband Joel. For more of Amanda's work, visit her blog at http://dulcinbradbury.livejournal.com/. Additionally, you can read her microfiction horror story "Crackle!" at *Tweet the Meat* (http://twitter.com/tweetthemeat) and look for a poem of hers in an upcoming issue of *Scheherezade's Bequest* (http://cabinet-des-fees.com/).

Deacon Carter's Last Dime

Nathan Crowder

Deacon Carter smiled like not a day had gone by and asked if he could use my yard to build his rocket ship.

"Boy, you're out of your goddamned mind!" The phrase had materialized on my lips. It seemed like yesterday, not the twenty years it had been, that I sold him a box of crap we had junked in the yard out back. Toaster break down? Most people, they'd toss it in the scrap down at ol' Frank Coffey's lot and buy a new one. Sure don't cost much to replace. But Deacon had a way of fixing things that most other folks just didn't get. I took over running the yard for my pops, and then it was James Coffey's Junk Emporium.

And Deacon, well, Deacon got his brown ass off Washington Avenue about the same time, headed to college, and made a life somewhere other than the ghetto.

He just smiled up at me, all shy like. He stood there in the shade of the busted-up robot I had hanging from the sign of my junkyard. Wasn't much to look at, truth be told. All long and gangly, he was maybe a hundred-fifty pounds, soaking wet. Deke was wearing a t-shirt and a jacket that had a new kinda crispness to them, but weren't anything fancy. "Maybe I'm out of my mind, Jimmy, but I have to try."

I stared him up and down. Damned if he wasn't serious. "Come on in and we'll talk this over." I left the door open and shuffled into the dimly lit space that doubled as my office and living room, trusting he would follow me.

Over the drone of the ancient box fan in the window, I heard the creak of the screen door as he opened it to step in. I hurriedly cleared some unopened mail off the chair and brushed down the blanket which served as a cover with my hand. "Go on and have a seat," I offered. "You want a beer?"

Deacon slowed in his approach to the chair. "Beer? No man, that's okay. It isn't even ten yet."

I sucked on my teeth for a second, watching him sit. "I think I have some

66

wine..." I started. He looked comfortable enough, but this was a bit of a homecoming, and deserved some kind of celebration.

"Nothing to drink, thanks," Deacon said. He leaned forward in his chair. "I just need to know if I can use your yard. I'll pay you for the space rental, and buy any parts I need straight off of you, if you can find them."

I thought I had heard something about him working for this company out around Denver that made rockets for rich people. I thought it was a rumor. There couldn't be that many rich people needing rockets, could there? Kevin over at the liquor store told me there weren't more than a few dozen rich people who owned everything as it was. No wonder Deacon was back on the Ave. Prolly worked himself out of a job. "Huh...parts for a rocket ship. What you need a rocket for anyway?"

He sighed and sank back into the chair, deflated. "I thought that moving off Washington Avenue was enough, you know? I worked my ass off, Jimmy. I jumped through every hoop I could find, got into a good school and graduated at the top of my class. That guaranteed me a good career, and moved me into big house in the suburbs. I had it made."

I shifted uncomfortably on the sofa. I was feeling the cottonmouth, and longed for a beer. Should have grabbed one for myself when I had offered one to Deacon, but now I was stuck. I hadn't been expecting his whole damn life story. "All that good living done made you hungry for more or something?"

"Did you know most of the rich people live in orbit in private satellites or on the moon?" Duncan said. I must have looked surprised, because he was quick to argue his case. "They own anything of real value on Earth, and they don't even live here anymore. It's true. I've seen it."

"What do you know? Kevin was right about something for a change!"

"You think you know what rich looks like, Jimmy, but you don't. Hell, I sure didn't, and I've been a lot further than Washington Avenue." Deacon clenched his fist and pounded his thigh hard a few times. "I just, I didn't get far enough. The whole planet is a ghetto, Jimmy. And if I want out, I need to build a rocket."

"Now, can I use your yard?"

What could I do? Me and Deke, we went way back. Some might even say we had been friends once, before he got too busy for things like that. I gave him the spare key to the rolling sheet-metal gate, and told him not to worry about the Dobermans—damn things needed new hips, so I only had the motion sensor and bark-box active. I knew Deke wouldn't rip me off.

Everything back there in the yard was crap anyway, all ten acres of it. I kept it locked up more to keep bums from falling asleep in the discarded cars and fridges and then dying with the first frost. Bum stink was bad, but nothing compared to finding a ripe one two weeks after the spring thaw.

It wasn't like I expected much out of this rocket ship of his. Not at first. Hell, for the first few days, all he did was put in this high scaffolding which he covered with tarps. Then he handed me an envelope full of cash for scrap metal.

Sure as Sunday morning, there he was the next day, carving up junker cars with his two sons—twins named Arron and Abram. Each piece vanished beneath the folds of the tarp, with only the ghostly light of sparks through the canvas to show welding within.

Way I figured, I had a pocket full of cash and there weren't no reason not to spend it. It was more than enough for a few nights on the town with some champagne down at Mr. Lucky's for me and a few lovely ladies. It even bought me a shiny suit with matching hat, and I don't got to tell you the ladies love that! Less than a week later, I was back to 40 oz cans of malt liquor from the corner store. My only entertainment was sitting on the sofa watching courtroom shows, and the only one touching my balls was me.

I started getting interested in what was going on out back—even took to locking up the shop during the day and watching the scaffolding from my back porch. It wasn't as exciting as Mr. Lucky's, but not much is. Not to mention that it was a hell of a lot cheaper.

The rocket began to turn into a family affair round about the third month. Deacon's wife and daughter started to come along with the men. Mrs. Carter insisted on being called Elle. She was a plain-looking woman with tight cornrows and a fondness for workman jumpsuits. Their twelve year old daughter wore her hair up in two puffs on the top of her head and trailed her mother like she was the woman's shadow. I didn't catch the girl's name, but I think it was something like Cree.

While the boys worked the metal, Elle and Cree wandered through the yard stripping wires—bales of the stuff. Then Cree would sit in the dirt and go through the wire inch by inch, taping up cracks in the casing while her mom tinkered with instrument panels they had either found or brought in with them.

Some days they would bring Deacon's mother along. She shuffled through the gate like a little, black beetle. One of the boys brought in her folding aluminum rocking chair. She would sit in the shade in a rocking chair, alternating between reading and singing gospels, shifting every now and then to keep in the shade of the rocket as the sun moved through the sky.

I knew Deacon's mother from way back, but hadn't seen her outside for years. The crick in her walk made it look like something was wrong with her hip, like my Aunt Denise who lived somewhere in the Ohio sprawl. If Ma Carter still lived in the same sixth floor walk-up I remembered, her hip would explain why she rarely went out. I expected Deacon or his burly teen sons carried her out when she came to the yard.

When watching from a distance began to get a little dull, I wandered down to keep Ma Carter company. I had at least some history with her, and it wasn't like she was doing much to contribute to the rocket building. At first, I'm not sure she recognized who I was, likely the Swiss cheese memory of old age making her distracted.

"I've got me a good boy there," she said, her heavy-lidded eyes fixed on the rippling gray canvas of the tarp. She turned a silent eye to me. I couldn't shake the feeling that she was judging me by her son's measure and finding me coming up short.

"Deacon and I grew up together," I reminded her. "We were in the same class."

She stared, unblinking for a few moments, like a snake. Then a smile twitched up the corner of her wrinkled face and she patted the back of my hand with her dainty palm. When she spoke her voice had a vague sing-song quality, like she was going to break out into a hymn any moment. "That's right! Frank Coffey's boy. Don't mess with Coffey or you'll get creamed."

I laughed awkwardly. It had been years since I had heard that phrase— probably not since the old man's funeral. He was real proud of that. No one messed with Frank or he'd cuff them around, even if they were family. "That was a long time ago," I said, anxious to change the subject away from my childhood. "Some wild idea your son has, building a rocket."

She beamed a radiant smile at the mention of Deacon. "My son says there's a place on the moon where everyone is finally free. No slaves and no masters, and the only glass ceiling is the one keeping the air in," she said. "He's going to take us there. He's going to break the cycle."

"The cycle?"

The smile faltered, and she got dead serious all of a sudden. Ma Carter stared at me for a long moment, her gaze unwavering. "Did you end up finishing school?" She finally asked.

"I finished seventh grade and dropped out during eighth." I felt no shame over it. God only knows I wasn't the only one. Most of the kids on Washington Avenue didn't finish school.

She nodded, unsurprised. "Didn't you want more than this? More than running your father's scrap yard?"

I looked around and shrugged. "Dunno. Feels like I always been here. It's what I know. I'm not like Deke. I never got the same breaks."

"What kind of breaks did my son get?" Her eyebrows had been meticulously plucked then penciled thinly back. One now arched in surprise.

The way she stared at me, I was reminded of when I was a kid and said a curse word around grandma. Like, I had done something wrong and only barely comprehended what it was. Sweat beaded at the back of my neck under the old woman's scrutiny. My shoulders pulled up around my ears, my eyes shifted to find somewhere safe to land—anywhere but on Ma Carter. "Well, school and such—the teachers always liked him better. And then after school, getting handed a good job..."

"James Coffey, no one ever *handed* my boy anything! He earned everything that came to him, ten times over, by working himself to the bone. The teachers *liked* him better? Boy, they *liked* Deacon because he treated them with respect. He listened to them and he did the work."

Out of the corner of my eye, I saw veins straining in Ma Carter's neck. Her head thrust forward threateningly. Damn, I was going to get the old bird all riled up and it was anyone's guess which of us was going to die first. I was afraid that she was going to shake apart with anger. Or maybe she'd just pop a blood vessel and keel over. I heard that's what killed this ol' man who lived down the street. But she might just take me out with those bony elbows before Jesus called her home.

I caught sight of Deacon's shadow making his way across the yard. I don't think I've ever been so happy to see him as right then. "Ma, why don't you go help Elle with the instrument panel?"

Her anger dissipated at the sight of her son. An easy smile appeared so quickly, it was hard for me to believe it hadn't always been there. "Baby, I don't know anything about instrument panels."

Deke pointed off across the yard to where the girls had set up all the gauges and stuff they had been tinkering with. "She just wants someone to let her know when they light up. She needs Cree under the cabinet with her holding the soldering iron, so you'd be a big help. Elle will tell you what she needs." He helped her up by her elbow. He stooped to put his head near hers, damn near folding himself in half to do it.

Ma Carter squeezed her son's arm, and after a withering look over her shoulder at me, she shuffled off to help. "I can't believe you want to bring that one along with us."

Deacon looked slightly embarrassed. He watched her go, mopping at his glistening face with a folded up do-rag.

"What's this about taking me along?" I asked once I was confident Ma Carter was out of earshot.

"About that," Deacon said slowly, "There's going to be room on the rocket. I have more than enough space for the family. Some of my friends want off this place just as bad as me, and they're coming with us. I still have one more seat, if you want it."

I felt, I don't know, groundless, like I was fit to faint for a little bit. I never thought much beyond this scrap yard, let alone beyond Washington Avenue. Me? On the moon? I couldn't even imagine it. "Oh Deke, that's awful nice of you, but I don't know what I would do up in space."

"Jimmy, you can do whatever you want to do. You get to be your own man there, with no limits, and no one holding you back."

Now here's the thing—I know I should have been overwhelmed by the possibilities. I mean, the mother-fucking moon, right? My needs, my routine, it was too…earthy. I tried, I really did, to stretch my mind to bigger dreams. It had been so long ago that I really had any dreams at all. It was troubling that I couldn't remember them. "The moon…" I said, drawing out the word to buy time. "Must be like a big party round the clock."

I saw something in Deke's eyes, a softening at the corners. His smile dimmed somewhat. "Well, yeah, Jimmy," he said. "Except there isn't any alcohol."

"No drink? How about weed? I bet they grow some amazing skunk up there in space." I didn't need him to answer. His smile cracked and fell even as the words left my lips. "No, I guess not."

Deacon stood there for a while, trying to find the right answer. I saw him start, the words rising up to the back of his throat to be stuffed back down. Two, three times he started to say something. It must have frustrated him something fierce, because I could swear I saw his eyes go shiny, like he was about to cry. "Jimmy, you don't...we'll be on the moon. You won't have to escape anymore."

I'm not proud, but I saw red at this, this talking down to me, this *'Jimmy just gonna go hide from his problems'* bullshit. I been hearing it all my life. I was sick of it. The last person I wanted to hear it from was Deke. I thought we were beyond that.

"You know what, Deacon? I don't want a ride on your goddamned rocket. Thing probably won't work anyway. You're gonna blow up in my yard and I'm gonna have all kinds of explaining to do. The government gonna have to come in here with mops to clean you off my walls."

I turned away and headed back to the house, thinking the conversation was over. Leave it to Deke to get in the last word. "We're putting in the engine and propulsion drive in two days. We'll run a few tests, and hopefully leave within another three days. You have until then to change your mind."

I stood on my back porch and looked into the darkness of my home. I waited until I heard the sound of him walking back to the rocket before I turned around. Damn you Deacon Carter and damn your fool rocket.

I didn't bother going out into the yard after that. True to his word, a big engine-looking piece of hardware showed up on the back of an antiquated flatbed truck two days later. The three coffee-colored fellas who delivered it stuck around and helped maneuver it under the tarps with my grav-jacks. I watched from behind the blinds in my bathroom. The truck didn't move again, and I began to realize that the people who brought the engine probably had seats on the deathtrap hidden behind the tarp.

More people showed up on the fourth day, a dozen in all, trickling through the gate with bags and boxes. Some of them I knew from Washington Avenue. Most of them I had never seen before. They hauled out sawhorses and whatever flat scraps they could find to build improvised picnic tables. Food appeared, brought from home kitchens, or from restaurants around the Ave. It was a feast, a damned revival. There must have been thirty people down there. Everyone was carrying on like it was the last night of their lives.

As things were really getting going, I saw Deacon peel off from the group and step up to my porch. I watched him vanish beneath the porch roof from the second floor bathroom. He must have knocked and called out for a good five or ten minutes before he got the hint and went back to his party.

I watched them for a long time, aching to join them—knowing that I couldn't. Oh, Deacon would have welcomed me, no matter how mad that made Ma Carter. But they had something that I just didn't get. There was bounce in their step. There was celebration. There was...I don't know what it was. It

71

beamed from their faces, from their every motion. And it unsettled me horribly.

Sometime after they retired back under the tarp, I went downstairs. Deke had shoved a fat envelope through the mail slot. It sat there, propped against the door. He had been using a lot of metal, lots of wire, so maybe he was just paying me for it. Maybe it was him trying to buy my forgiveness. I didn't know. I collected the envelope and hefted it in my hand for a few minutes. It felt heavy. I fished my penknife out and slit the envelope open along one side. That was a lot of green in there.

I was standing across from Kevin at the package liquor store fifteen minutes later. He gave me a nod of recognition. "Same thing as always, Jimmy?"

I patted the lump of envelope in my jacket. It felt wonderful and heavy. "Not today, Kevin. It's top shelf from now on."

"From now on? For reals?" Kevin narrowed his eyes. I had waved a few bills around the last time Deacon paid me for use of the lot. He must have known that was long gone. The idea I might have more money from Deacon was a very real possibility, and I know he was thinking it.

The shop was quiet this time of night. There were only a few stumblebums back near the rotgut, counting collected change and doing math. I pulled out the envelope and fanned the bills so that Kevin could see. It felt good to have that much money.

The size of the bankroll started to bother me a bit. I hadn't counted it, but there were big bills there. I could work my entire life, sell the scrap yard and the land it stood on, and I would never see that much money again. Not that anyone would want to buy that dump anyway. With this kind of money, why should I stay on Washington Avenue? I could move somewhere nice; maybe get a quiet house in the suburbs. This kind of money…

…this was Deacon Carter's last dime. He must have sold everything, cashed out his savings, and put every dollar in that envelope.

There was no reason for him to do that unless…unless.

A flash of white paper tucked among the green of bills caught my eye. I dug around in the envelope until I found it. It was a note, in Deke's handwriting. He had scrawled it on the back of a bank receipt, confirming the closure of his accounts, which I had already suspected. I read and then re-read the two simple sentences. "Thank you for everything. I won't need this where I'm going."

My hand shook as I folded the note. I hurriedly stuffed it into the pocket of my jeans. *I have one more seat, if you want it,* Deke had told me. Hell, I still didn't know what I would do if I were on the moon. A whole lot of nothing, I reckon. I turned from the counter so quick, I almost knocked over a display of cheap gin right behind me. I paused long enough to steady the teetering green bottles before I hustled out the door at something just short of a run.

Within a few blocks, I noticed people standing out in the street. There were the faint echoes of a distant roar, bouncing down the decaying brick buildings, and the residents were pointing to a brilliant new star in the sky, receding away from Washington Avenue. It didn't take more than a few minutes before it was lost in the haze of light pollution. I knew what they were watching, even if none of my neighbors did. I stopped running and fell to my knees on the sidewalk, oblivious to the smells of urban decay and the sounds of wonderment.

Sure, I had the money to get off Washington Avenue. I could move away from the stumblebums, and the smell of urine in the doorways, and the trash blowing down the street. But money couldn't buy my way out of the ghetto, and Deacon knew that. His words from that first day rattled around in my head. *The whole planet is a ghetto, Jimmy. And if I want out, I need to build a rocket.*

I stopped crying soon enough. Wasn't anything I could do about it, anyway, and a grown man crying in public like that was foolish. I dried my eyes with the back of my hands and started back to the liquor store. On the way, I pulled out Deke's note and read it one last time. A wind blew up Washington Avenue, and I let it pluck the note from my hand and whisk it away down the sidewalk. "To Deacon Carter," I said as I watched his words cartwheel into the darkness. "Hope you get where you're going."

Nathan Crowder is the author of four novels set within the Cobalt City Universe: *Chanson Noir, Cobalt City Blues, Greetings from Buena Rosa*, and *Ride Like the Devil*. His short fiction has appeared in such places as Thuglit.com, *Byzarium, Crossed Genres, Absent Willow Review*, and WilyWriters.com.

Nathan resides in the Bohemian wilds of north Seattle, where micro-brew beer flows like water and everyone wears ironic t-shirts and goatees – even the women. He lives alone with his cat, Shiva, who is currently managing his career in exchange for fresh kibble. Online, he resides at www.nathancrowder.com.

The Strangler Fig

Jennifer D. Munro

We'd never spoken until today, except for the day she named me long ago in a backstage hallway. She had crouched to tie her shoe, and roadies bumped the black-haired backup singer as if she didn't exist. Only I saw her. I snapped her: *click*. Her head snapped up at the sound. *Click*, she mimicked the camera's voice, a voice I throw. She worked an air shutter. I shuddered, newly baptized as Click.

Then, when I developed into her shadow, I became Click the Tick. I was in two places at once. I followed her career, and flashed it ahead of her at the same time. With my photos, I made Kiara, and she made me.

Click the Tick, her tongue castanets. Click the Tick, her fingers snap. Click the Tick, her heels on tile. Not only do I cling tight; I measure time, her second hand. I count.

But we don't talk to each other. One does not expect conversation from one's deity. One expects lightning bolts. And Kiara delivered, turning me with one syllable from ordinary Thomas, nerd with a telephoto, to Click: best of the celluloid infantry. A man worthy enough to have a nickname. Loners are never called anything but what's on their birth certificates, called out in medical waiting rooms and at airport gates. Until they become unhinged and acquire a pet name. Unabomber. Killer Clown. Jack the Ripper. When they see their new moniker hit the papers, they know they've become somebody, important enough for re-christening.

I can't forgive her when she disappears like this. Every year, the same time, up in a puff of smoke. Before she vanishes, she starts to cover herself up like a virgin fundamentalist, and her voice starts to crack. I could never pinpoint the date's significance—not her birthday, not the solstice, not the anniversary of her Mexican grandmother's death—but I've learned that tomorrow marks the beginning of the annual Huichol pilgrimage to Xapa, the Tree That Rains. The villagers have begun to file out in droves, heading for the peyote ceremony to get fried in the name of extinct gods.

The Strangler Fig

Before her annual evanescence, Kiara refuses interviews or performances, claiming laryngitis. She hides behind sunglasses, scarves, and baggy dresses; the baby bump rumors start. She takes a new lover. Then she goes underground, untraceable. She reemerges a few weeks later looking fresh and young, bikini-clad and gorgeous, her voice sliding up and down the range of a piano as easily as hands do. The rags crow that she's gone under the knife. These know-it-alls know *nada*. I know every crease of her flesh better than my own (no one wants to look at me, including myself). I am her microscope. No knife, no injection, but...something.

Flawless, like last year around this time, at the gala benefit—for cancer, or animals, or animals with cancer, who gives a rip, we just care about the gowns and gams—*Mi ácaro*, my tick, she mouthed silently to me and blew a kiss. Then turned away, into the microphones of the yakking interviewers.

But I don't hear. I only see. Freeze-frames parade through my head, as if I look at a contact sheet instead of at the chaotic mob. First: Her sandaled toes peek out through the cracked-open limo door. No nail color, ever. We glimpse her long, sepia leg—no stockings, always bare skin, one of her trademarks. Then: a pause. We intuit the whole of her, complete entity in the dark and cool interior. We stare, yearning, as funereal congregations gaze upon the coffin, knowing what's inside. We sense the pearled and powdered beauty beneath the mahogany slab.

Then comes the heel, ankle, calf, nudging open high skirt slit, my life's meaning thrust through a stage curtain. So like her tongue through her lips, taking her time, teasing. Then knee, thigh. A hand. A twist at her waist, unseen. Then Kiara. We receive the whole of her, but we never get enough. Not even with the backless dress, tease of drapery and miracle of architecture cascading from threads at her shoulders, offering us the entirety of her spine. Each vertebra, count them, fulcrum of her grace. The wisp of cloth waterfalls beneath her sacrum, sacred seat of her soul, god-made indentation for a man's palm to guide her—but no man will. This she proffers to us, so much more profound a revelation than pedestrian cleavage heaving along the catwalk.

Amidst the perfume and hairspray and sweat, her natural fragrance shimmers: nutmeg and mango and oak-barreled whiskey. Chocolate and chili. All simmered into the essence of her skin.

Most paps don't work the red carpet. After all, the paparazzi get top dollar for the shot of stars with their clothes off, not their makeup on. We want the wrinkle, the wart, not the de la Renta. But Click'll get the candid of her that everyone wants (Kiara checking, over her shoulder in the limo's reflection, the transition from skin to silk just at the swell of her tailbone, a mere millisecond). All the other hacks with single lens reflex stand in the same place, with the same equipment. But blind.

Just a few weeks before that, I caught her on an icicled balcony in the middle of godforsaken nowhere, 1000mm and F2.8 all the way through, grainy but solid gold, unmistakably her despite the sunglasses, ushanka, and white mink coat swaddling her up past her chin. The tabloid editors say *Christ, Click, how'd you know? How'd you get the shot?*

She'd sprinkled none of her usual clues for me to follow. She cuddled with a new lover (cropped out), descendent of some Svalbardian prince, or so he claimed. His Highness soon disappeared, though his absence never hit the U.S. papers—we don't care much for the fate of jaundiced, bottom-runged nobility. An alleged accident on the way to his hunting lodge. It seems that his Stolichnaya-fond majesty had always been careless near crevasses. Poor out-of-the-frame prince, wedged into his gorge of snow like a pallid lemon slice. Shaken like an ice cube, his dentures chatter and clatter in that great martini glass in the sky. But who knows if that's really how he met his maker, since the body was never found?

Then Kiara lost me again, as I knew she would. I'm sure she, too, was shaken when the photo hit the checkout stands, and she realized I'd tracked her without the calculated hints she left for me throughout the rest of the year. I'd sniffed her out despite no phone bills left in her garbage, listing calls to her next destination. She knew I'd cropped out the only evidence that paired her with the wan prince.

Along with the digital shots I take for the pimps who sell my work to the highest bidder, I shoot film—high and low speed, 35 mm and 4x5, color and b/w, long and short exposures—for my experiments. I pondered Prince Icechip's frozen image under my Agfa Lupe. Why him? Anodyne, disinherited scion won't be missed. No thorough inquiry. Lost himself *on the rocks*. A shrug, case closed. Still, a poor specimen. Kiara has slipped, skittering over the edge with an elbow called *time* at her back.

She resurfaced in L.A. for the gala, once again looking as if she'd bedded Father Time, nudging back his hands. So gentle, turning over this mythic, snoring bed partner without waking him, so that he doesn't know he's rolled back the clock in his sleep. Dark in her new tan, even her eyes seemed darker, the whites tinted, like her image had steeped too long in fixer bath. Stiletto-heeled starlets, starving over salads and suffering under the knife, clutch skinny soy lattes by her poolside, begging for her secret. She confesses with that impish, ever modest smile, that she's blessed by her genetics. A little relaxation, a little *amarosa*, and food of the soul, a recipe passed down from her ancestors—and here she pauses over her enchilada, smothered in mólé, the traditional dark sauce that Latina grandmothers take three days to make with a hundred secret ingredients—all work wonders for an overworked girl. She could say *goddess*. Say *star*. But she says *girl*, as if she were still a waitress in Cleveland who had need of a surname and a phone book listing.

She knows I'm there, watching through my telephoto, her shadow at noontime, underfoot but unseen.

But not today. She doesn't know I've finally tracked her to this filthy Mexican town. So this is where she goes when she ditches me every year.

I wait in the cemetery, City of the Dead. *La Ciudad de los Muertos*, I say out loud, killing the time, but I make a hash of it, as usual. I cannot master my own tongue, much less her adopted one. The words are clear in my head, but they tumble out of my mouth like scree down a talus of shale, all clatter and squawk.

My telephoto points across the small bay to her house, perched on a rock outcropping at the north end. Behind me, the graveyard's haphazard, angled headstones look as if they erupt from the mounded earth, not as if human hands lodged them there. The jungle creeps nearly to the ocean here, and the strange trees that lurk around the graves creak and groan as the branches rub together. Strangler Figs, requiring sacrificial host trees of a different species to wrap themselves around. I had asked my hotel proprietress about the peculiar, tentacled trunks. The host tree eventually dies, mummified in the arms of the Strangler.

The Stranglers' dry leaves whisper in the sibilant wind. Crones chattering, clicking their tongues, tsk tsking. They scuff their gnarled toes, shy and tall ladies wallflowered behind me, waiting to be asked to dance. They skulk and scuttle. But when I turn to face them, they haven't moved. Their canopy blends together, like schoolgirls holding hands overhead, singing *Ring Around the Rosy*. A massive Strangler towers over the others, most likely the mother of all the other trees, sending out vines that snake down doomed host trees; the aerial roots encircle the helpless tree and fuse together to become daughter Stranglers. I lean against a coarse, latticed trunk; my hand comes away sticky with a dark pus. Wasps cluster around the bitter fruit.

Hummingbirds levitate near low bushes, pollinating as they suck up oleander dew that would kill a man three thousand times their size, *click click clicking*, mocking me as I wait for her. Even before dawn like this, the hot pumice air grinds me down. A dry scraping hasps at my ankle, a skeletal caress. The roots form into fleshless hands, winding around my Achilles heel and up my shin.

I start awake, kicking. I must have dozed standing-up, leaning against a Strangler. A small branch snags my sleeve, and another scratches down my collar. A prehistoric-looking beast, the size of a newborn baby, crawls over my foot. It hisses at me, frantic pulse visible in its corded neck, then thrashes away through the underbrush. Just an iguana, mistaking me for a tree in my khakis and camo vest. I swipe at the prickles left by its thick hide and move to the tideline, washing him away with the sting of salt water.

It makes its ungainly way up the shore of Moth Bay, *Bahia de Polilla*. I follow it in my viewfinder until it disappears beneath the sudden onyx of her skirts close in my sights.

Covered up like a Biblical virgin, all Jackie O shades and glimmering veils and robes, she's still somehow ripe with curves and supple secrets under the shapeless drapery. She moves between me and the burial ground and rasps, "*Ácaro*," the first word she's said out loud to me since that fateful day backstage two decades ago. Her voice seems abraded by incinerated bones, as brittle as the papery husk of dead moth's wings. Nothing like her usual velvet butterfly voice.

Jennifer D. Munro

She mimes pulling a swollen acarid from her scalp and flicking it away. But she can't get rid of me so easily. Such careless removal leaves the tick partly-embedded and contaminates the host. Ticks require gasoline and fire. Only hellish conflagration removes us.

I snap her: *click.* She grabs my camera. I don't resist her. We're never this close, and I smell her skin, though I've barely noticed the dank, whale breath smell of this Mexican town that the few off-season tourists gripe about. Fingers under their noses, they flee north, where the sand is infested with fleas, but they prefer bites to this unholy stench.

Sucking waves lick at our feet, leaving green-tinged foam on the hissing sand. Seaweed litters the dingy shore in gnat-plagued mounds. A crow-like bird caws on the sodden mass, a masticated-looking clump. Three turkey buzzards peck at a fish carcass—the fishermen here gut their *dorado* and *huachinango* immediately and dump the carrion on the sand. The buzzards pause to look up at her, then return to their grisly work. Their beaks *click click click* on dorsal bone.

The smell of her overpowers the ocean brine and decomposing sea plants, the fetid jungle and mulching cemetery. But instead of wanting to pinch my nose, I yearn to chew her odor like cud. Beneath the yeast of her lurks a spice that tingles on the tongue.

She pops open the catch and yanks out the film, then shoves it all back at me. Her fingers brush my hands. I'm never privileged to touch her. But I've seen the goose bumps that rise on her lovers' skin. Hers isn't the warm maggot touch I would expect in this tropical germ whorehouse, but is the icy touch of a princess asleep for centuries on her crystal pallet. My sense of her is always only of sight. So today, with smell and touch, I'm satiated, as with the sex I only have with her photo collage and my own hand, a decoupage tryst.

"You shouldn't have followed me here." Her voice grates like a rusted lock.

I don't mind that she's destroyed my morning's work. It's not like I could sell these photos of her looking like a war widow, unrecognizable in her weeds. I stuff the exposed negs into the darkness of my bag, where I'll save them for my experiments later.

She whirls around and creeps back up the inlet, returning to her *casa* on the jagged bluff. The thatch-roofed, adobe manor lords it over the tiny, high peninsula of cragged black rock. She moves slowly, as if she aches. Her black form climbs the steps, past the terraced gardens, past the pool, past the large palapa with its umbrellas and lounge chairs (where her latest man-boy, whom she ignores, dozes).

I follow her with the telephoto, one eye shut to all around me, the other eye open only to her in the crosshairs. She looks like a scarab, an injured beetle that continues to limp along, making its crushed way toward its final destination despite being one of eight legs away from death. She crests the top step and passes behind the cratered walls surrounding the house. Rows of arches form the walls—like skeletal eye sockets stacked in catacombs. The skulled arches are too

78

small for a man but let in the breeze. And mosquitoes. And celluloid, an almost impossible shot from daylight into darkness. Almost.

Dingy stucco, grimed with dust and time, slathers the strange walls. A domed and thatched roof rises behind it. Support beams at haphazard intervals thrust up through the dark straw and pierce the sky, hinting of heads speared on dungeon gates.

As she disappears, she doesn't even glance my way. I am shut out, like a lens cap blotting my sight of her. I imagine her standing in the mottled darkness of her temple that I was never meant to see. If I could manage a complete picture of her behind this bank of blank eyes, I imagine it would look much like the pieced-together collage of her on my bedroom wall. But instead of being assembled from chopped-up film squares, she would be dissected by these gaping ovals.

The malicious sun breaks behind me and washes her out.

Her boy stirs; she's called to him. He lifts his designer sunglasses.

Kiara's voice. How could a planet, a nation, a man, help but fall under its spell? She flirts with octaves as she toys with lovers like this palomino colt, foolish braying boy with his golden skin, sun-bleached hair, and nothing between his mule ears.

Sad to think that—unlike the Stradivarius, whose song remains ever beautiful through the centuries, deepening with time into mournful eloquence—the human voice must weaken and falter, soundtrack to the lines and sags that must eventually mar our skin. Unlike the strings of that fabled instrument, our vocal cords cannot be replaced. Not an ageless instrument composed of wood, but mortal, with sinews and synapses that rot and atrophy.

The boy, dressed in a skimpy Speedo that doesn't bother with his rump, stands up and crosses over to the pocked wall. Straight-spined, no shame or hard work to weigh him down, he left a trail of brags about his famous mistress, all too easy to follow. Who knows how old this preening donkey is? Twenty? Thirty? Hard to tell now that I've passed forty and then some, and she's not far behind me though she still looks just beyond jailbait. Youth all looks the same to me now, bland, like this new crop of bare-bellied hoochie girl singers who can't touch Kiara's talent or beauty; you can't tell them apart except for the Kool-aid streaks in their hair that I want to yank. So easy for me to pollute their images with the shots I manufacture, their disgrace smeared across the checkout stands.

The boy, this spoiled pony, kneels in front of the cat-holed wall. Kiara's panicked, grown careless to allow his unbridled mouth. He reaches through an opening, his scapula flexing as his arm disappears up to his shoulder. The other hand reaches between his own legs. I know he paws under the folds of her shrouds as she stands on the other side. Thinking he fondles a creature who looks like the poster in his gym locker. She hasn't wholly given herself to him, yet. She makes them all wait, until they have little sense left when the time comes. Their last glimpse of her must paralyze them.

This little display is for me. *Not you*, she's saying to me. *Never you.*

Jennifer D. Munro

I cap the telephoto; she sees my eye blink closed.

The boy's hand drops free. Even from here, I see his fingers rise to his nose, see the snap of his head, turning away, the hand snapping in the other direction away from his face.

Put it in your mouth, I say out loud, but he kneels beside the pool and splashes it in the water, then dries it on a towel, rubbing until it's well past dry.

*

Developing film has been almost impossible in this sun-drenched town. Dust, salt-laden air, and Cancer's Tropic light all leach through door seams and window cracks, infiltrating even inner rooms, like the ants and cockroaches. I can't darken even the back bedroom or bathroom, but I manage to stuff myself into a closet and feed the negs into the metal roller. I cap the lid on the canister and move my wrists, not rapid like a bartender's, but smooth like a dancer's, to agitate the developer evenly over the film. The solution is not one I purchase over a counter, but my own concocted recipe. It's taken a great deal of experimentation and patience to perfect the formula.

I've done this so often that I don't need a timer's beep to let me know when to rinse and fix. Trapped in darkness with the fumes, I don't need a red light to illuminate my task. The rattle of coat hangers at my back startles me, as if a cold hand taps me on the shoulder. I snap on the light, unsurprised by what I can already make out in the celluloid coils. Her image isn't there, of course, no residual ghost of her in her Bride of the Dead costume. Even the murky dawn light flashed her out, like a nuclear bomb would disintegrate a real person.

But the others are there. Auras of faces, mouths open, all of them, a hideous Munch canvas of tortured souls in each tiny square. I can see them even in miniature like this, though at first it was only in large blowups that I recognized the pixel-masses for what they were. Some of them I've come to recognize. Like old friends, they're there whenever I take such a picture. There: a jaundiced smudge that coalesces into an ignoble desperate for a tipple. Her new palomino pony will be here soon (but not soon enough for me), oh so surprised, faint at first behind the others, but staining deeper with time. The distorted shapes and splotches gel into discernible features. If I overlay an old shot of a lover's face (irrelevant mugs cropped out but saved, as I hoard everything she touches), I make a perfect match. Of course they've followed her here, too. They are always with her. Like me.

You might call me a stalker—obsessed, dangerous—except that it's my job to follow her. She is my life's blood, my income, my career.

Not psychotic. Symbiotic. She needs me as well. My lens raises her to mythic heights of beauty. She is my creation.

There are many of my kind, a dime a dozen making their bread and butter exposing the cellulite and transgressions of gods who should be perfect. The business of our pack is to smear the unbesmirched. To mar what is sacred.

80

The Strangler Fig

But there is only one Kiara, posed on her holy pedestal. My eidolon. Only one of my kind can destroy her, burn her image, and turn her to ash in the public mind's eye. But she knows I never will. To smash my idol would be to destroy myself.

On my bedroom wall back home I had assembled her graven image. Craven, distorted collage: breast, hipbone, elbow, knuckle, snapshots in skewed angles captured through windows and doors. I staple gunned pieces of her to the plaster. It took me years to acquire the surreal whole, every inch of her, nude, life-size. Four walls: front, back, both her sides. I see her through a fly's eyes, compound images multiplied densely and divided into myriad squares—right side up, of course. I studied it as I fell asleep and awoke. Not my bedroom, but my laboratory, my own psyche pinned to the plaster.

In the hazy state of half-sleep, I started to see things.

Another face. Not hers.

Then: another.

My own jealousy, I thought, of the men who'd been inside her, while I'm perennially outside, always her surface: skin, curl of hair, lay of a dress. To touch her nostril or earlobe would be enough, but they've been inside the chalice of her. Don't say the vulgar word you're thinking, the clinical word. This she does not have. What she has is holy.

If I stood back and looked, as at a museum painting, they weren't there. Only as I looked away, or fell asleep, did I see them. Like the Rorschach images burned into the eyelids when you close your eyes after staring into the sun. Like the green flash as the sun sets on the horizon that you're never sure you've actually seen. Glaring magenta screams behind my Kiara.

I began to test new methods. Infrared lenses. Sun filters at dusk. Noontime ASA film at midnight. A flash at noon. Millisecond or 32-minute exposures. Pinpoint cameras and coated lenses. Dodging and push processing. Half-developing negatives. Reciprocity effects and reticulation. I've never tried completely exposing the film like this, leaving not a trace of her latent image. But the trapped lovers remain, unwilling ghosts nattering at her back. More clear than I've ever seen them.

Maybe it's this place and not the process. The graveyard sulked behind her.

*

Long ago, I gave her a photo of herself. A gift left outside her dressing room, shared with other nameless backup singers, a black and white she could use to promote herself, still plain Kara Grealy. I included a caption: *Kara's Chiaroscuro. Love, Click.* I heard her asking someone for a dictionary. I gave her the negative, too, one of the few no-nos in my line of work. I'd like that negative back, because I know what I'd see behind her: nothing. Just my Kiara. No stains.

Then she disappeared. *Poof.* I hit the bottle. She reemerged a year later as simply Kiara. So you see, I named her, too. Exotic creature, her own fabulous tapestry woven from the frayed threads of her mixed and murky lineage. Her name needed no further appellation. Like Jesus. Mary. Lucifer.

She was suddenly fluent in the language of the Mexican grandmother she now claimed—a woman she'd never met, a country she'd never visited, until summoned to her deathbed, or so goes her most famous ballad. I dried myself out, bought a Spanish translation dictionary, hired a tutor, worked diligently, but words don't roll easy on my tongue. Some I can manage. Photo: *foto*. Film: *membrana*. Naked: *en carne*. Same as meat: *carne*, my line of business. *Sin tu*, without you, a sin. But I stumble over words. Speech is not my method of communicating. I lip read better than I talk. I smell a false trail more easily than I can recite the *Pledge of Allegiance*.

Like the mólé of her adopted country, she took a hundred separate ingredients and used her secret, inherited recipe, boiling them down into one dish—her new identity. I backed it all up. I documented her made-up truths, turned her lies into reality. The fame that had eluded her until then exploded like a supernova.

Year by year, she's grown darker—though her skin is still smooth and unlined—easily explained by sun worship, though modern actresses have given up this pagan ritual in our cancer-riddled times. But I know that she draws her curtains to *el sol* and casts her devotion to the moon. Her skin can only be the pigment of her grandmother calling from the distant past.

I want to be part of the fabric. Not apart.

Not what I am, a bedbug on the linen, despised irritant.

Not what I am, always witness, never in the frame.

Not what I am, one of the mongrel pack who chase her, like the hundreds of stray dogs that crowd the pitted streets of Moth Bay. All descended from just a few lost pets long ago, the hotel proprietress, a transplanted gringo, told me. Like the townspeople themselves, all descended from just two ancestors: a Huichol priestess and the first Catholic priest to land on this shore, a man of the cloth who disrobed to lie with her. I see hints of Kiara when I look at the villagers. They won't talk to me, even when I stutter out an *hola* at the *mercado*. Secretive, as tight knit as the jungle trees. They say it was the women who saved the town from slaughter when the conquerors invaded. The white men simply disappeared, one by one.

The Moth Bay dogs ceaselessly hump each other, copulating though they're nothing but sacks of ribs and mange, as if they had no choice but to mate, a last ditch effort at immortality. A spastic, robotic rutting lacking in joy—like me and my hand and my photo collage. The proprietress warned me the townsfolk will set out poisoned meat tonight, as they do every year at this time, a ritual cleansing before the pilgrimage and influx of tourists. Tomorrow, before dawn, a noose of dead dogs will be tossed into the ocean. Tied tail to neck, tail to neck, in a distended necklace of bloated corpses, surreal killick that anchors this town to a medieval notion of purging its incestuous plague. The lariat of carrion will rock gently beneath the surface, so easy to tangle an ankle and be sucked down to doom. The water will turn filthy with jellyfish, feeding on the swollen bait. But no matter what the town does to eradicate the dogs, the proprietress says, they return and multiply, a virus. They reincarnate themselves, refusing to be exterminated.

Like them, we paparazzi exist on the margins, fighting each other over scraps of humanity. We're punched and kicked, flipped off, wished dead. The masses spit on us but buy the snaps we take, starving for more. We hound the perimeters, hated, but without us, the fiction falls apart.

The spool of film crackles in my hand. I stumble from the closet and bump into Malele, the maid's toddler. She follows me everywhere. Malele's dress is dirty, her upper lip encrusted with dried snot. Her mother trails me through the house, sweeping after me, making me uneasy. She leaves cleanliness in her wake, silent except for the *flap flap* of her rubber slippers and the *swish swish* of her broom.

Malele and I have been teaching each other the names of colors. We point to the deadly oleander: *pink*. To the sleeping grass that snaps its leaves shut when touched: *verde*. To the prickly *guanabana* fruit that looks like an angry blowfish: *green*. To the bumblebee drowned in the pool: *negro*. To the poisonous angel's trumpet flower: *amarillo*. We argue over the ocean's color: *Azul*, she says. No, not blue, gray. To my hair: *blanco*. It turned white overnight, when I saw the faces—not from horror, but with terror that we would grow further apart as I aged while Kiara remained unchanged. A gecko *click, click, clicks* at us: *brown*. Malele stomps upon it with her bare foot. It scampers away, leaving its tail, and she runs after it. I pick up the gecko tail and carry it outside, flinging it onto the sand, where the rich insect life will make short work of it. The gecko will grow another tail, a nifty trick of rebirth.

A hammock stretches itself between two coconut trees. Erosion of the beach has exposed the skirted black roots of the trees, shameful like a widow's slip showing. A bulbous, black termite nest hangs in one, a malignant tumor. The termites' tunneled tracks scar the tree from the inside out, an old man's raised and scabbed veins, but the termites shy from light and won't cross the whitewashed trunks. I shed my many-pocketed vest and lie in the hammock. She'll know I'm no longer watching, the third eye closed. A skinny horse nearby strips a banana tree of its leaves, its grinding molars audible even over the constant, hammering waves. The harsh sun blotches the back of my eyelids. Inside the coconut trunk, the termites' busy drone lulls me into *siesta*.

Kiara approaches me on the beach, scarab skirts crackling around her. A mantilla, flowing from a tortoise shell comb, falls over her shoulders. She peels back her webbed veil, peels back the skin of her lovely face, revealing a travesty of decay. My Canon has captured the slivered hints of her deterioration just before her annual donning of full vestments. Her nose, earlobe, the corner of her lips: rotting like a leper.

She climbs into the hammock and tucks the gecko tail behind her ear, a flower that grows reptilian limbs. The ocean froths behind her, beating its fists against the pebbles and shells, which chatter and clatter with each grasping wave. Her long nails tap, a beetling *click click click*. Castanets of my soul. Scrape scratch tease the inside of my skin, palms and shins inflamed with her inside me. She crouches over me, her back to me, astride me, so graceful the hammock doesn't rock. I pry the comb from her scalp and run the mantis-limb prongs through her hair. She tips her head back, her black hair brushing my chest, scampering ants tickling. Her wet hair drips. Dark water stains my nipples, leaves tracks down my belly, pools in my navel. Her hair oozes, pungent unguent, an urgent seeping. Smell of damp mulch, a gold-bearing alluvial soil. Black secretion, amnion seething, leaching weeping coils in my fist, dripping ink tattooing my hide. Black dye. *No*, Malele points, shrieking. *Roja. Sangre* drips down my cheek. I poke out my tongue to lick, to taste the brine of her, but feel a tickling instead.

I thrash awake, nearly tossing myself from the hammock, and pluck a dying termite from my lips. Termites live only one day, long enough to mate and destroy. It's nearly sunset, and my fingers cramp around the cold black lens that I'm never without. A moth *click click clicks* against a porch light, hurling itself against the impostor moon.

Seaweed pops and sizzles, cooked by the sun and now cooling. While I've slept, I've lost my shade. My pasty skin is now red—outlined by the white shape of the camera on my chest—my body too used to scuttling in the night, covered by vests and baggy pants, layered with pockets and pouches—to hide things in, to hide myself behind, to secrete. I'm sure the hammock ropes indent my back like a chessboard.

I am a game board. Play me.

Kiara moves down the beach, real now, still in her nun's garb. Beside her, the flaxen pony frolics in white briefs (aptly named in his case). He ignores her, running to retrieve a child's ball and dancing in the waves. With them, an old woman. They creep toward the graveyard. The green strobe flashes as the sun sets.

I will not follow. I'm tired.

When I was young, I chased butterflies. Caught them in nets, spread and pinned them, displayed them in boxes. Good practice for what I do now—study, capture, still the moving subject, frame. Only to find they were all just moths, every last one of them common pests. Their identity mattered, though their outward beauty hadn't changed. Like a candid of a has-been or of a beautiful nobody—worthless. Now here I am, burned out in the cloying heat of Moth Bay. Poetic justice. Full circle. God has a sense of humor.

A rusted pickup jounces along the hard-crusted beach. Its tires pass over a dead gull fanned out in the sand, pressing feathers and bones beneath tread marks, leaving a trace of shocked shape. The creaking, squeaking truck crawls past, crunching the seaweed. *Camarones! Camarones!* An old man in the pickup bed squawks through a loud speaker that amplifies and strangles his words. Translucent and veined shrimp dangle from strings stretched across a high bed frame. They dance with the lurching truck, synchronized like sickly chorus girls lifting their skirts, spindly legs tapping together. Their exoskeletons brush each other, *click click click*. Dust and flies chase their ghostly, fetal bodies, but each heaving bounce keeps them from settling, skittish. The old man gives me the once over, leering recognition in his eyes. A look that all of the townspeople seem to give me.

Tough day for business. Besides the stench, no one can swim because of the dark tide, an influx of toxic seaweed. Like the riptides, no signs announce the danger, no newspaper articles, no lifeguards. But there is Kiara, a dark silhouette, unmistakable to me, cleaving the dark water, a kelpie drawing the unaware to their own doom. Lemmings, the early tourists will dive in if they see another swimmer, assuming their safety.

She seals her way back to her promontory. She thinks I'll pace her on the beach, like the iguana paralleling her on the sand, its flailing gait leaving thrashed tracks. But I sit tight.

She climbs out of the water up onto the rocks at her crown of land. Even at dusk I see that she's lost her nun's habit and is naked, her lithe body haloed in the crepuscular light. She emits her own corona. She disappears behind the apertured wall.

I heave myself out of my webbed cradle and turn the other way and walk South towards the City of the Dead. I leave my camera in the rope net.

I'm used to working at night, but the darkness here is complete; no refracting neon brightens the sky like a hippie god. *La luna*, gorged on light, hoists its full belly over the top of the towering Strangler Figs and washes the jungle in a pale glow. The arms of the enveloping Stranglers shroud the slivered ghosts of the host trees.

I touch the smooth bark of a host sapling no higher than myself but with much better posture. A gust rattles its bleached leaves, sending a shudder down its shimmering, golden trunk. Quite a lovely tree, really. Just behind it, a Strangler Fig reaches with murderous arms to hug its trembling limbs. Long roots have just begun to unfurl themselves from the canopy to coil around its outflung branches, grafting themselves around the slender trunk and knotting themselves together in a callused embrace.

I break off a branch of the palomino sapling with a vicious snap. Dark sap flows from the wound. I taste it, bitter, and feel a mercury shock in my veins, a paprika tingle on my lips, a rancid-meat nausea in my belly. The over-arching canopy stirs, setting off a dry whispering of leaves. A bird caterwauls.

"The sap dries up too soon," she says from behind me. I'm not surprised that she's there; I smelled her, her earlier scent of rotting mulch now gone beneath her usual complex myrrh. Her familiar velvet voice violins down my spine, with no trace of her earlier clawed tones. "They're not strong enough to survive." She points to an anemic stalk nearby that's caught in the maws of a giant Strangler Fig. Wooden bangles *click, click, click* on her smooth arm. Gone are her vestments. Dark nipples tinge her white halter top, as does the triangle of dark hair beneath her tiny, white shorts. She looks younger than the day I first saw her.

The thick Strangler hide wraps itself around the pallid host tree and soon will completely shroud the pus-colored torso and all of its blanched leaves, joining itself down the middle in a long scar. "This one can't take the heat. A transplant too used to the cold."

"Maybe he just needs a vodka martini." I emphasize the *he*. She smiles at me, not startled that I'm flitting near the truth. She wants me to know. She must. She wanted me to follow this time.

She places her hand reverently on the Strangler. "Gracias, *Abuela*," she murmurs. She strokes a knobby protuberance on the sallow trunk in the Strangler's grasp. The tree crackles, leaking out a meager black sap that she catches in a clay bowl. She licks her finger, and the clock of her face ticks backwards.

I would stand here forever, voluntarily, to feed her needs, to be inside her like that. No, I would kneel.

"I can give you what they can't," I say, too close to begging. I have what they lack: patience, endurance, persistence, desire. A knack for camouflage and standing still. And no other need but her.

"A daughter," she says. "But it requires a strong will. As the years pass, it takes more and more to sustain me. These have no stamina. To have a child, it would take an exceptionally hardy—"

I interrupt her, afraid she'll say *specimen*, not *man*. "There's truth in the power of a man who chooses his fate willingly for the one he loves." I don't use the word *sacrifice*, for I have nothing to lose.

"Yes."

She's known all along it would be me.

We are moral equals. Or should I say immoral equals. Stopping at nothing to freeze time. We belong together.

She points to a tombstone wedged into the rooted knees of the largest Strangler Fig. There's no sign of its original host tree, long since sealed completely within its massive trunk. "My great-grandmother," she says. "*Bisabuela*." She's looking at the tree, not at the grave.

She steps towards me. She takes another lick of the black sap from her bowl, and then she kisses me, tasting of acrid electricity. My knees almost buckle, but I hold myself up as she backs me toward the *bisabuela* tree. She slides her shorts down and presses against me, reaching for my fly.

Out of nowhere the iguana appears at my feet, its thick hide identical to the tree's bark, and it winds its way around my ankles; I can't distinguish between its tail and the roots. "Grandmother looked just like me on the day she passed over and passed on the gift. Though some call it a curse. My own mother refused it. Fled to a new country. These souls, they're hollow, but heavy. I'm tired, too, Click." Her bracelets echo my name as her hand slides up and down, a friction, a fissure broken open.

The Strangler Fig

I'm naked. Inside her. I can't tell where the tree behind me ends and Kiara, enveloping me, begins.

To be like this, always.

I picture the relief.

I stand in one place, for all eternity, welcomed into the bosom of her family, waiting for her to come to me for her sustenance, knowing someday I'll be wrapped in her arms forever. No longer scurrying after her, a rat sniffing her scraps. My boughs forever extend out to her in eternal welcome. My obvolute fingers caress her as she strokes me. She needs me as never before, to nourish her. Me, the key ingredient to her mólé—spectral treacle. She stands with her chattering sisters, the *azul* beach framed behind her. Tourists spy her under the protective canopy. *Look!* they cry. *Kiara!* Kiara, who had retired and gone underground in search of peace, quiet, family.

She graciously poses for them, still looking like a girl of twenty, standing against a tree, a babe cradled in her arms. The infant looks up at the swaying branches as at a cooing father. The tourists snap her picture.

Click.

There I am. At last.

I'm in the frame.

Like the others, my mouth will be open. Not in horror, but in joy.

Jennifer D. Munro grew up in Hawaii as a fourth generation islander but now makes her home in Seattle. Her grandfather slept through the bombing of Pearl Harbor outside his bedroom window, but she's an insomniac who writes when she can't sleep. She is an Assam tea addict who can't handle liquor well, but she gives it her best shot. She breaks cars and computers with astonishing frequency.

Her work has appeared in more than fifty publications, including *Best American Erotica 2008 and 2004*, four volumes of *Mammoth Book of Best New Erotica, Thou Shalt Not: Stories of Dark Crime and Horror,* and *The Bigger the Better the Tighter the Sweater: 21 Funny Women on Beauty and Body Image.* Her short story collection is entitled *The Erotica Writer's Husband.*

Author's website: http://www.munrojd.com.

The Bat and the Blitz

Erika Tracy

Never in the field of human conflict was so much owed by so many to so few.
-W. Churchill

David Johnson returned the salute of the guard beside his office door and entered, not sure what to expect. Within, a familiar figure sat in David's chair; he was sorting a few slips of paper, pushing one away and pulling it back. "Uncle Vlad!"

The older man looked up and grinned through his whiskers. "How military."

David grinned back at his godfather and took a seat on the corner of his own desk. "Air Command isn't that picky and you're not that official. Tell me you brought friends."

The old man lifted a finger and concentrated briefly. The papers vanished. "They will be along shortly. You understand this is strictest secret, and so does the Prime Minister, yes?"

"Of course. He's more than a little nervous about it, to be honest."

"So am I. But we can save many people, many factories."

David had never asked his godfather too many questions, not that he could remember. He knew the other man had been born in Russia; he knew that his own parents had taken in Vladimir Galkin as a young refugee in the last war. He knew that the older man hated the Germans with a dangerous passion. At this time, for this purpose, that was enough to know. "They will not hesitate at killing people to save people?"

"I think not. They are true Empire soldiers. And for my part, I have no qualm."

"I don't know why warlocks can't serve openly."

The old man smiled a little. "Because today's soldier may be tomorrow's uprising. They feel that the less we know of fighting, the better. I – I have read

88

bad books."

"For tonight, they are not bad. Not for tomorrow night either."

A knock sounded at the door, cutting off the budding philosophical discussion. David would have regretted this, but the shadows were growing. There was little enough time to put everyone in place. David was just grateful that warlocks could be mobilized with such remarkable speed. "Come in!

Six slim black-clad figures walked in, not quite in a march, each with a staff in his left hand. The first drew the eye, a natural leader, taller than the others and square in his shoulders. At Vlad's nod they lined up neatly for David's inspection.

"Charlie McBain," the first said, holding out a long-fingered hand to shake. "David Johnson."

And down the line. Samuel Bunter. Gilbert Ladbrooke. Mordecai Wolf. Franklin Thomas. And... "You're a girl!" David blurted. Somehow he'd assumed combat magic would require a man.

"A witch," his godfather intoned, but David barely heard him over the girl's self-introduction. "Batty Nattie, at your service!"

Her smile showed all of her teeth, her jaws slightly parted. Batty indeed, he decided; in a moment of boyish bravery, he had once caught a bat, and her smile reminded him of how it had shrieked into his face. "Pleased to meet you," David offered.

Thomas laughed. "Natalie Wyndham if you want to be formal about it, eh, Nat?"

"Well, yes, if we're being formal an' all."

David turned to Vlad and arched an eyebrow. "Careful," the older man said. "She'll bite your nose off."

David was absolutely not going to back up a step as if he believed such nonsense, though the girl's sharp teeth made him want to. "Very well. I need one of you each for Southampton, Southend-on-Sea, Bristol, Reading, Glasgow, Belfast, and I wish I had ten of you for London."

Vlad looked a little surprised, but nodded. "I shall take London. The rest of you? Remember, keep your heads down. Don't let *anyone* see you. Miss Wyndham, you should take Southend. Behave yourself and stay out of sight. David, keep an eye on her."

She seemed perfectly capable of keeping an eye on herself, and David had hoped to be in the air. They were shorter of planes than of pilots, though. He could let someone else fly his plane tonight if it would make Vlad happy. It didn't make the girl happy at all, judging by the twist of her mouth, but she wasn't going to argue with her old teacher. He wondered if she was the one most likely to spill secrets or do something a little too colourful. "There's a nice covered spot near the coast, good and far from civilians. You should be able to see whatever you need from there."

"Covered spots 'ave a way of becomin' uncovered." Still, she came with him.

"I don't suppose that's a Travelling Cloak," he said of her floating cape.

"Nah."

"We'll drive, then, and fast."

"Or I could meet ya."

"Master Galkin said to stay together."

She had no argument for that. They arrived without further discussion and found a quiet tree-covered spot with a view of the ocean. "Pity to waste such a nice night," she observed.

"With luck, it'll stay this quiet," David said, already knowing it wouldn't.

"What about Liverpool?" she said suddenly.

David shrugged. "They'll have to make do with normal weapons. There aren't enough of you to go 'round."

"They come from there, right?" She pointed out over the water.

"Yes."

"So the more I take, the less for everyone else, right?"

He grinned to himself. "Right."

She gave a decisive nod in the growing darkness. "Good."

It showed good spirit, at least, but he wondered how many bombers one witch could account for in a night. If the German command chose a different line, she might have nothing to destroy at all – and he suspected she would be worse company for it.

It was nearly full night, and nothing had happened yet. David excused himself and walked away to visit a bush. There wouldn't be time for such things later, if all went as expected. He returned to the same spot he'd stood on moments before – and found no witch. A few confused circles later, he thought to look up, only to find a dim shape in the tree's upper branches, a pale face peering down at him. She was laughing, the silly woman. "Is this why I'm to keep an eye on you? So you don't break your fool neck before the Germans even get here?"

"The view's better 'ere. And I think I 'ear something."

A moment later he caught it too, a faint drone almost blending with the sounds of night. It grew. He could barely find an edge, a glimpse even as the noise raged almost overhead, just occasional darkness against the stars. He strained his eyes looking up, longing for a weapon.

Something blue-white rose from the edge of his vision, racing up, spiralling a little. An instant later its trail vanished into a burst of orange and roaring explosion overhead. He threw himself to the ground reflexively, counting seconds until the wreckage would hit. Watching from below the sturdiest-looking branch, still low to the ground, he saw the largest flaming bits come down a little further along the flight path.

"Cor! Liked that," he heard her announce proudly from the top of the tree.

"Bloody hell, Nat!" he shouted back. "Remember the bits come *down*!"

"Forrard an' down. Don't'che trust me physics?"

"Mental," he muttered to himself, knowing it would be lost in the roar of aircraft. A moment later another pale blue streak shot up to find a target. This time the explosion was much smaller. He dared to get up and dust off. "Fighter!" he shouted up.

"Bombers are better!" she called, and fired again.

"And none of them are ours!"

She didn't answer that right away; she was busy. Again and again the blue-white rocket came from the tree. He had little to do but keep an eye out for anyone approaching on the ground and wonder if the spell smelled like lightning. He may have imagined the crisp tingling feeling in the air. In a lull, she told him, "I wouldn't 'it one of ours."

"We should move. They'll start trying to hit you soon."

"Just a jiff." She did something he couldn't see through the red streaks in his vision – he'd looked up again a moment too soon. He heard a slapping leathery sound, blinked around for its source, and missed it. A moment later, the girl stepped from behind the tree, surprising him. "I only fire on the ones with this." She drew something in the air he guessed was supposed to be a black cross. "The spell won't burn anything else."

"Clever."

She grinned as though she'd invented the whole idea of spells herself. "Where to?"

"A couple of ridges over, maybe. They're starting to skirt here, see? Even if you could get them from here, there'll be a fighter run on us any minute."

She didn't dawdle. He thought that, at least, showed a little sense. From their new position, they watched the ground torn to bits where they had stood. "I don't suppose you can hit them without the trail all the way from here to there."

"Sorry. And there's a real one – there." She pointed with her staff to what seemed to him just another patch of the roaring night. The light rose, engulfed, and consumed. This time he could hear bombs exploding within the blast of the plane. In the glow, he could see a fighter swerving too late, taking burning scrap into its engine, and tearing itself to bits. "Rather dull, really."

"*Dull?*" He'd rather be in the skies himself, piloting one of the fighters, instead of standing here with nothing to do but watch this mad witch. Still, he didn't feel that anything with explosions, bullets, bombs, and spells could rightly be called dull. He was beginning to smell woodsmoke, petrol smoke, and hot metal from all around them.

"Could be better." She casually shot down another plane with an accuracy any gunner would envy. "Back in a jiff."

He blinked at her. She gave him another toothy grin, lifted her staff to horizontal, and flattened it to a medallion between her hands. "Won't you need that?" he started to say, but before the words were fully out, he no longer spoke to a woman. A large bat flapped before him, then rose upward into the night. This was probably the sort of thing he was supposed to have prevented, though he had no idea how.

He didn't know a lot about magic, though perhaps a bit more than most normals. He did know that there was no way Natalie could cast spells in that shape. She could get hit with a stray bullet, or sucked into an engine, or something equally pointless. She could –

The blue-white streak stabbed downward, or so it seemed, a little distance away. A moment later, it struck somewhere else, from the side. He tried to judge what she had hit from the size of the explosions. She had certainly done some damage. In the evening she'd taken five Junkers, a Heinkel, and at least two fighters – no, three, he corrected. She'd earned a medal. Whole squadrons often did less in a night.

She couldn't have one, of course, because the only thing more dangerous to the country's well-being than admitting a warlock could do the work of several heavy guns was admitting a witch could do it. Even the most anti-warlock Englishman had a softer attitude toward witches just for being women, but that could change in a heartbeat. Nat would have to keep her pride secret in her heart instead of worn on her chest. Vlad would have told her all this, and there she still was – another plane spiralled down, its wing destroyed. She was still fighting for her country, with no prospect of reward unless she counted the relief from dullness. What was she doing out there?

At least they didn't have to worry about retaliation from Germany's magic-users. There were none.

She returned after a few more minutes of mysterious fire. This time, listening for it, he heard the whispering sound as wings. She fluttered in his hair, probably just to annoy him, came to rest, and rose from the ground to stand before him, a witch once more. "Good?" she asked.

Her hair was tangled into a fright; he could see that much even in the dark. He had a sudden mental picture of her flying up, turning back, and casting spells as she fell freely through the air. The black cloak draped on her shoulders was no parachute, though he supposed it might slow her a little. "You're bloody mental."

He could see her teeth flash in that alarming smile once more. She shrugged a few times. "Good, then. Shoulders are a bit sore."

"Popping out of freefall into flight? I should imagine."

The smile's edges turned up into something a bit more pleased and less menacing. "Clever bloke."

He pictured it for a few more moments, lacking anything else to do but watch her stretch, twist, and occasionally strike at another plane. "It's more fun watching someone who can miss."

"Is it? Besides, I *can* miss." She said this as though she'd have to work at it. "I should think you'd rather be up there bein' the one who can miss."

"I would." He eyed the sky, gauging the roars of the engines. "We should move again."

"Back to the old bit?"

It wasn't a bad idea in theory. "It's on fire."

"Well, then. Somewhere else." She sounded as though she was doing him a favour. He wondered if she could walk through fire.

He drove them on a bit farther, finding a new squadron for her to tear apart. He wondered what the German pilots were making of this new weapon. If any parachuted out, he might find out. He wondered what his fellow Fighter Command pilots were thinking. If he'd been up there, his thought would have been "Thank heavens."

"Penny?" she said as he yanked the machine to a halt.

"Thinking what it would be like to be up there while you're the latest weapon."

"You do fly, then?"

"Usually, yes." He didn't add the thought that nagged at him: *When I'm not babysitting a witch for no reason at all.*

"It's amazing up there."

He waited for her to add something. She didn't. "Of course, I'm wearing an airplane at the time."

"Can you see them?"

He shifted on the seat to try to look at her. His eyes had grown used to the dark, but her expression was unreadable.

"The other pilots, the crew. Can you see them?"

He took a deep breath. "I don't look."

She nodded. "They're tryin' to kill us."

"Exactly."

He heard her bracing herself, and then she opened the door and got out. He followed. There was a lull in the noise, leaving them alone in the dark. She was leaning on the car looking up.

"What do you do when you're not flying?" he asked her.

"Lately? I'm a warden. Neighbourhood's almost forgot I'm a witch, unless someone's leg wants 'oldin' on." He nodded his understanding. "This's easier."

"Is it?" He was a little surprised. He hadn't thought about the jobs people were doing on the ground as he tried to defend his country from the air. He'd wondered a little about the firemen, because the fires below had demanded his attention, but from above it was easy to forget that the square structures and the fires had people in them.

"The first time they hit near me, I was on an errand. The building in front of me swelled up like a bloody balloon, showered glass everywhere, and went square again. I got blown right backwards. And that was when I became a real warden. I had to walk forward while everyone else was running away, and I had to wrap up bloody bits and dead babies who'd been blasted out the windows. What are they doing, taking a bloody fag break? Get over 'ere, you bastards." She addressed that last to the horizon, which obligingly filled with planes once more.

"Another wave. Be careful what you wish for. And stay on the –" *Ground,* he'd meant to add, but once more she transformed herself and flapped away. He wondered what it would be like to be in a dogfight up there without

93

the plane, just falling and flying. He wondered if anyone had managed to see her, and if anyone did, whether that pilot would believe what he'd seen. He wondered if her accent always faded a little when she wasn't being deliberately annoying. Thinking about her was easier than wondering if he was strong enough to face a dead baby launched from a window by an explosion.

On the horizon David could see searchlights; right where they were, there was only Natalie, taking the enemy before they were expecting conflict, where there had been a small hole in the British forces. Here, Natalie was enough.

This time when she landed she was panting. He hadn't brought water, but he did have a small flask of brandy for emergencies. She had a sip, then made a startled sound. "Strong stuff, mate."

"Don't drink and fly. Unless, of course, you have to."

"I'll stay down a bit. Knackered."

"Don't wear yourself down. We may need you again Wednesday week or tomorrow night."

She dropped her head for a moment, her chin on her chest, her bush of tangled hair falling forward. "I'll take Wednesday week, thanks."

"I'll let the Fuhrer know your wishes directly."

She laughed, and without breaking the laugh or looking up jabbed her staff upward. A plane overhead erupted.

"Nat?"

With a sigh, she muttered a few words. Flaming metal bits rattled and slid from a dome that had not covered them moments before. "Picky bastard, aren't ya?"

He thought of six things he might say to that and elected to say none of them. She shoved back his flask. He had a little. "I don't hear any more."

"I do. They're going–" She pointed out to sea. "–that way."

He wouldn't argue with the hearing of a bat. "They're running."

"They're out of ruddy bombs." She offered a few foul words on the subject of Nazis, impressing him.

"Will you marry me?" The words popped out before he'd had time to think them, never mind censor them for any of a thousand good reasons.

She stared at him for a long moment, probably thinking of her own thousand good reasons. "Ten children, mind. And my own cat."

"Poor cat," he said in the same automatic way he'd said nearly everything to her tonight.

"If y'always spoke without thinkin', Galkin wouldn't have done this project with you," she mused. Her expression suggested he was a blouse she was thinking of buying. "Any witches in your family?"

"My mum."

She walked completely around him, looking him over and adding to his doubts. Now he felt like a horse at the market. Any minute now she'd check his teeth and fit him for a saddle. "Where's your family from? It's not any bit of Britain I know."

The Bat and the Blitz

"Mum's from Russia, Da's from Rhodesia."

"That explains a bit." She studied his face for a long moment. "All right, then."

"Is that a yes?"

"It's a 'we'll-see.'" She leaned against him and hooked her arm through his. "Ask again once we've lived through Wednesday week."

He was taller than she – barely. He had time to think about this, provided they did live through a few more days of fire raining from the sky. "No. We're getting married before that."

"And you called me mental for falling among the Junkers?"

He quested back in his memory of the night. "No. In strict point of fact, I first called you mental for showering us with falling Junkers, but you're close enough."

She looked around the flaming ring of debris she'd shielded away. Luckily she'd also shielded the car; a large chunk of metal flared and sizzled a few feet from it. "I don't know I can marry a man so fond of stayin' alive."

"You want ten children, you'll need your man to stay around a while."

She shrugged, which felt nice against him. "Should we go back?"

"We should watch a little longer. Sometimes there's a predawn wave."

She offered a few more fine words on the subject of Nazis, fighter planes, and bombers.

"Do you think Vlad'd be my best man?" To her blank look, he clarified, "Master Galkin, I suppose you're used to calling him."

"Assuming a bit, aren't you?"

They stayed until the eastern sky paled, watching the sky. In the distance bombs still fell; they could feel them almost more than hearing them. One of the last planes glowed, catching the morning sun in its smoky exhaust. To David's trained eye, the black smoke looked like someone had scored a hit. "Out of range," Nat grumbled.

A spirit moved in him, tired as he was. He bounced to his feet and shouted after them, "And stay out!" Nat giggled. "They never bloody listen."

"I guess we report back now?" Nat asked, the last word scraping on the front edge of a yawn.

"Technically, you all report back to me, so I'd best get to where the rest of you lot can do that. Ready?"

"Is it far? I lost track."

"Not far."

"Good. I'll use the loo there, then."

He felt himself blushing. If she really did marry him, if they really did both hold to his mad impulse, then such intimate details would be commonplace.

They were the first back to Hornchurch. He waited in his little office for the others, startled by each and relieved. Vlad returned fully an hour after David and Nat, covered in soot and with his clothes torn. "London," he said briefly, "will stand. Where is Ladbrooke?"

"Not back yet. Should we wait?"

"He took Bristol. I will search. The rest of you, sleep, I suppose, and prepare to be called again."

David caught Nat's eye. Their news could wait until Ladbrooke was found, or longer, if it had to. It could wait until the deed itself was accomplished if she liked it that way. Once more he imagined her falling through the air, casting her spell and grinning in her wild way, and his heart leapt. Vlad looked around the room before he left, his gaze lingering a moment on David. "Bristol," David said. "The rest of you can sleep. I'm used to doing without."

Some things came first.

Erika Tracy lives in Georgia with her husband, too many dogs, an outnumbered cat, and a no-longer impending baby. She holds degrees in philosophy and music. After writing fantasy for years, she is now letting other people read it.

Just occasionally, she writes about dogs at http://sniffydog.blogspot.com.

The Good Old-Fashioned Kind of Water

Camille Alexa

It rained eight days and nine nights without stopping. It rained and rained, the tattoo on the metal roof reverberating along the cabin's iron framework of poles with crusted joints. It rained and thrummed and spitted until April thought her ears would bleed. When it stopped, its sudden absence was deafening.

· April lay in the black night listening to a thumping she slowly recognized as her heartbeat. Scattered on the lodge floor like rotting logs or lurking crocodiles adrift in a swamp slept the others: her brother, her three younger cousins, the redheaded twin Johnson neighbor girls who'd been sent up to higher ground with them when the bio-bombs turned the clouds green and the caustic rains first fell on the valley below. Their slight breathings in the absolute darkness could have been the sound of shushing snakes, or the scrabblings of blind mice.

Trying for silence, April stepped over sleeping bodies. Outside, beyond the steep overhang of corrugated tin keeping corrosive drippings from soft organic matter like the bodies of children, pale green threads of dawn streaked hazy grey skies. April tugged a pair of large heavy boots onto her feet. She lifted a rain cloak from a peg by the door, sliding it over her head with the pitted side out, mottled industrial rubber like molting bark.

Her boots squelched soft noises in the sucking muck as she stepped off the flagstone porch, the sluggish grey matter of liquefied ground eddying higher than her ankles as she slushed through it. Slimy overcooked vegetation, particulated minerals, the dissolving bodies of small wild animals overcome by the rains all swirled in her wake as she slogged across the yard toward the treeline at the rim of the clearing.

Branches dripped overhead. April drew the rubber hood close around her

97

face, glancing upward at brightening sky. Drip-drip-dripping echoed through the denuded forest with musical pit-pattering. Few trees had withstood the latest rains, fewer than ever before; fewer even than the time it rained four days and five nights. Then, at least a few trees had kept some leaves. Now the naked limbs prickled the dawn sky with skeletal branches.

April glanced down at the grey-green sludge. It deepened as she went, sucking halfway up her shins uncomfortably close to the tops of her boots. Inside, protected by enhanced rubber made heavy with industrial chemicals, her feet were cold; colder than night, colder than wet hair. Colder than dead people, of which April had ever seen only two up close.

Overhead, the bald pitted trunks of dead trees rose twenty, fifty, sixty feet into the air. Their bony twigs stretched toward each other like starving prisoners reaching through bars for food or comfort. Their exposed trunks, many stripped completely clean of bark, had bleached so pale in the most recent deluge they almost glowed in the filtered sunlight spilling over the crest of the ridge.

April had never seen the woods so naked. Sparkling beads of green-tinted rain dripped from high branches, bright as crystals from ballroom chandeliers, or emerald necklaces, or some other thing equally startling and beautiful. At the cliff's edge with its shallow caves at her back, April shielded her eyes against the glare of morning light glancing off thick acid droplets and gazed down into the valley.

Floods had turned what had once been the ridge of a single steep forested hill into an atoll-style island, surrounded by an ocean of sludge, with naked woods in the middle, a lagoon of dead trees. Little of the old farmsteads was still visible in the valley. The very top of the Johnson grain silo rose above the glittery mire. The roof of April's house was just recognizable, and the leafless crown of the massive elm that had once shaded the whole house and half the yard. Farther off was the listing tip of the old church steeple, and just beyond that the ruined crumbling ramparts of the broken dam.

April's bedroom had been on the side of the house nearest the elm. She imagined her window just beneath the surface of the lake. The bodies of her parents, too, and the dog Lancelot with the broken tail and the three-legged cat Mehitabel. She'd never tell her brother Mitch she pictured them all in the house still, as though they slept just under the slimy mineral surface of the swollen lake; or that she imagined the house just the same, except all quiet, maybe with the curtains swaying back and forth slowly in grey-green gloom.

She sometimes dreamt of her mother and father lying on their bed in the house under the corrosive waters, without their clothes or their skin or the meat of their muscles. Skeletons, lying side by side, bone arms crossed over bone chests. She didn't need Mitch to tell her that was stupid; the rainwaters dissolved anything they touched for long, even rock and metal. When she'd told Mitch the week before that the metal under their lodge's porch was dissolving, he'd threatened to smack her ears. He hadn't wanted to hear, either, that for the past few nights the freshwater well under the eaves had glowed pale blue—so pale, you could see it only if you stared deep into it after darkfall. It wouldn't glow if there was even a single candle lit.

But April almost never slept well, and on dark nights as quiet as if the others had all stopped breathing in their sleep, she'd crawl to the lip of the well, lift the plank cover, and stare down into the water until her eyes ached and bile swelled up into her mouth like slimy green floodwater swelling into the valley. Only then could she see the blue. During the day she tried not to roll her allotted cupfuls around in her mouth, tried not to taste the blue nighttime glow on her tongue mixed in with the good old-fashioned kind of water.

April jumped carefully from the top of the small rise to the rock ledge jutting from the cliff wall like the pouting outthrust lip of a stone giant. After eight days and nine nights, the scruffy vegetation habitually tufting from the limestone face in fist-sized clumps had completely disappeared. Here and there, slimy trails marked the recent dissolution of vegetable matter, and sometimes a naked woody root thrust at an awkward angle from the rock.

April reached the lower ledge at the rim of the valley, now a murky ocean of organic soup. From the waterline the church steeple and the Johnson's submerged silo looked smaller rather than larger. She squatted at the lip of the cliff, once halfway up the face of the ridge, an impossibly high climb from her house.

She and Mitch had hiked all over these hills when they were small, back when the clouds over the valley were the old shades of white and grey instead of the heavy greenish purple of unhealed bruises. The air at the edge of the flooded lake smelled like turnips, or perhaps raw radishes—but greener and sharper, with an under-whiff of decay.

She reached into her pocket for the metal can pressing against her thigh, hard as a cylindrical rock. Mitch would box her ears if he knew she'd borrowed a can-opener. She opened the can of green beans, slowly so as not to spill anything. Green beans packed in water.

Each child chose two cans a day from the thousands in the stockpile their parents had dragged up the mountain two years earlier when the threat of ecowar had first become big in the news. Mitch usually chose some meaty thing from the damp wooden crates: tuna or sardines or liver paste. The Johnson girls always picked sweet stuff—peaches in heavy syrup, or maraschino cherries. April took cans none of the other kids wanted, anything as long as it was packed in water: green beans, beets, asparagus, corn; other things she'd never heard of before, like water chestnuts, just for the word *water* in the name. Water wasn't the same as rain. Not since the ecowars.

April sipped metallic water from the can, floating green beans bumping against her top lip like the minnows that used to swim the lake. The old lake, not this one swollen monstrous and bitter.

Before long, the familiar bony fin crested the flat grey surface and sliced through grey-green fluid in April's direction, wavelets rippling outward across the sludge as the fish neared. The lake fish was so large—so *prehistoric* looking, like a thing from an old science textbook—she'd first had difficulty thinking of it as anything other than a sea monster. Except there was no sea, of course—just the rippling caustic expanse stretching from the ledge she stood on all the way to the ruins of the dam across the valley.

On the other side of the dam was another small mountain, now another island densely prickled with dead trees. Electricity disappeared when the first bio-bombs fell, scattering spores engineered to corrupt the air, the water, the soil, the human bloodstream. Lights from homes dotting the far hillsides had flickered out all at once the night the dam broke. April never saw any smoke or other signs of life from the houses during the day, but at night, if she squinted really hard and concentrated, she could see small pinpricks of blue glow, and softer, larger glowing patches, like fungus on a rotten log.

There could be someone over there across the dank green mire, eking out a life and making do just as they did. There might not be; but also, there might. And between that shore and this one the big fish swam, the sea monster with no sea but a valley flooded with the muck of acidic water and the molecular soup of dissolving dead things.

April stood as it surfaced. Its rounded bulk rose high above the sludge, one enormous eye bluer than forgotten sky fixed on her with a steady inhuman stare. The viscous green-grey liquid of melted vegetation rolled from its mottled rubbery hide, dark and thick and pitted as April's rubber raincoat. The fish rose with a strange muscular buoyancy to float on the muck: a treeless, mottled rubber island. If not for the fluttering gills, the fanning ray fins and wide, cavernous mouth—gaping and with a clownish downturn at the corners—she would've supposed it was about what a whale looked like. She'd never seen a whale in real life, and though the lake fish looked mostly like the groupers her father used to bring home for supper, its size made even larger aquatic beasts the more obvious comparisons: whale or sea monster, either and neither.

April drained the last water from her can around the edges of soggy beans, her mouth filled with a coppery tang even sharper than acid-laced air. She chewed one bean slowly, then flipped one to the sea monster, which caught the thing on its large protruding shelf of a jaw. Its movements were subtle, seemingly accidental, though the bean landed in the exact center of the creature's mouth, which remained open. April could easily have convinced herself it hadn't moved at all if she hadn't seen it a dozen times before.

She stepped to the ledge and said, "Sorry I couldn't make it for awhile. It was raining too hard. Maybe you can go out in that stuff, but I can't. I'm glad you enjoy green beans."

That section of the cliff had always been steep. It was easy to imagine the sharp drop-off immediately beneath the ledge; a drop-off steep enough to accommodate the bulk of a fish the size of a fat bus. April leaned out over the water and extended her hand, and the creature swiveled a blue eye as she stroked its thick hide. She ignored the pain of her burning skin where drops of lake sludge clung to her fingers, blistering them red as she watched.

The Good Old-Fashioned Kind of Water

She shared the rest of her beans with the animal, alternating one for her, one for it. It had no teeth to speak of. It was powerful enough, big enough, to be a creature that swallowed things whole rather than tearing off chunks. Twice, the fish closed its wide jaw like a drawbridge, taking in water and decaying flotsam, and when it opened again the cavern yawned empty. Inside arced ridges of cartilage, the arches of an organic cathedral. The sense of something powerful lingered just out of sight past the fish's gaping mouth; something capable of crushing bones and pulverizing sinew and gristle.

April finished the beans, careful to eat with the hand she hadn't used to pet the giant fish. When the food was gone the creature shimmied its tail. Its gills rippled half above, half below the water.

"Are you sure you want this can?" she said, looking at the peeling label. "You liked it last time, but it still doesn't seem like a good thing to eat. Not to me, anyway, though I guess lake fish sea monster whales are different. Okay, then. Here."

April patted the fish just beneath the globular blue eye, then stepped back and tossed the empty tin can along the same trajectory as the beans. The fish made no noise as its jaws closed like a sprung hinge.

The animal sank from view, mottled hide blending into murky grey-green sludge even before it submerged completely. Bubbles broke the surface where it had been, but April no longer felt the heavy presence, the thickened air pressure and weight on her inner ear that always accompanied the beast's presence.

"See you next time the rains break," she murmured to the expanse of brackish green, the surface calm and unbroken all the way to the listing church steeple.

It took longer to make her way back up the mountain than down. The earth soaked up the rains as the day warmed, making the ground more slippery than ever. All organic matter had melted from the chalky hillside, and the minerals of the soil itself were beginning to dissolve.

Mitch blocked her way as she stepped in off the covered porch.

"You can't take the best cloak and boots," he said. "What would we do if you wandered off and broke your leg? How would we get the stuff back then?"

He'd been angry even before the bio-bombs, unable to go to college last year before the ecowars hit so close to home. It wasn't April's fault their parents hadn't let him leave the valley, though he'd always taken it out on her more than anyone else.

"I didn't break my leg," she said.

He snorted. He took a swig off the whiskey bottle from the crate only he was allowed to touch, since the rest of them were *too young*, he claimed, though April sometimes felt far older than he was. "You won't find anything out there, so you might as well stop looking," he said, wiping his mouth on the back of his wrist. "You, always dragging home lame one-eyed dogs and starving cats with broken tails. Well, there's no animals in the valley to save anymore. No people neither, so you might just as well forget about it."

"There might be people. And there's the big fish in the lake," she said. "It's an animal and it's living out there, so there could be more."

"Shut up about your mutant fish. Those stupid stories make the littler kids stay up nights thinking something big's going to come out of the floodwater and eat them."

"It likes green beans just fine." She lowered her eyes and finished removing the boots and cloak, placing them carefully on shelf and peg. She joined her cousin Sam and his sisters in the corner of the cabin, where they slapped cards one after the other onto a cleared spot on the floor like spiritless automatons. They played the same game all day every day, some game they'd devised between the three of them, with convoluted elastic rules producing no satisfying outcome April could ever see: a game that never ended, just dragged on and on like rain drumming on a metal roof.

Later that night, everyone but April and one of the redheaded twins vomited, cramps low in abdomens tight as drums. They'd all had their cupfuls of glowing blue water, except April, who hadn't drunk from the well for days. One of the Johnson twins had always hated water, even the old-fashioned kind that fell from white clouds and tasted clean. Her skin was so pale and thin April could see her veins running blue beneath.

That twin sat next to the other one, holding the red hair from her sister's face as she retched into an empty jar. The other kids groaned and rolled on their mats, and Mitch drank whiskey until he passed out even with cramps. April imagined she saw glowing blue water pulsing through their bodies, as clearly visible as the blue veins in the redheaded twin's wrists.

They fell asleep one by one, crying. April spent the night going from each to the next, assuring herself they still breathed and wiping sweat from their cheeks with a dry cloth. In the morning they woke feeling better—all but Mitch, who had to be shaken groggily awake, and the sick Johnson twin, who didn't wake at all.

Mitch was furious about the dead Johnson girl. He shouted wordless rage, and kicked over crates of canned food, ignoring the tin cylinders rolling beneath his feet with their colorful paper labels of mandarin oranges, of organic chickpeas, of condensed milk. He cried, and tugged his hair, and opened another bottle of whiskey and shook April's hand off his arm.

"It's not fair!" he said. "I could be in the city doing something useful; not stuck here with a bunch of kids and a thousand cans of random tinned crap making me sick."

"It's not the food, Mitch." April refilled and righted the last crate and shoved it back against the wall. "It's the water. I told you, it's blue at night. Maybe it's another bio-weapon making its way to the valley from the rains, or soaking through the soil into the well."

But Mitch threw his nearly full bottle at her, which narrowly missed her head to smash against the rough-hewn lodge post behind. She knelt to pick larger shards off the floor and put them in her cupped hand, sharp whiskey tang stinging the insides of her nose.

Her brother looked vaguely apologetic for a moment, smaller and younger, like when they were little. But then his mouth hardened around the edges. He stomped to the rain cloaks by the door and thrust his feet into oversized boots, muttering, "And now I have to go dig a grave in this muck, even though a body would melt faster above ground than below."

They buried the Johnson girl just past the first line of naked trees. Back in the old days, when April and Mitch used to hike up to the lodge each summer to camp with their parents, the bushy undergrowth and low ferns made the cabin feel secluded. But now, with all the leaves and green stuff washed away, the remaining Johnson twin was clearly visible where she stood under the rippled tin awning, her arms crossed over her breasts. Her translucent skin glowed in the late afternoon light, making her a pale ghost-child with dark hollows for eyes.

That night nobody drank water from the well but Mitch, who fell clutching his stomach, flailing blindly and yelling threats at anyone trying to help him. After he drank himself to sleep, April eased the bottle from his slack fingers and measured out the remaining whiskey into tin cups for the rest of them, though the oldest of her cousins wasn't even twelve. They spent the evening digging through the thousand cans by candlelight, pulling out whatever struck their fancy long into the blue-tinted night.

…*Tell us again about the big fish in the lake of the valley*, the smaller kids whispered around slurps of sour whiskey sweetened with the syrup of canned pears.

…*Tell us again about the blue lights on the mountain on the other side of the dam.*

So April told them again about the mammoth whale monster grouper fish with its mottled rubber hide, which rose to the surface of the murky floodwaters above their old homes to accept her touch on its wide clown-jaw and revel in the taste of green beans and tin cans. She told them for the dozenth time about her idea: about letting the great animal carry them to the mountain across the valley, where there might not be more people, but there might be.

The Johnson girl hadn't spoken since her twin's death. She stayed curled next to Mitch, staring at nothing as the camping lodge's metal poles and foundations groaned the pained grating squeals of fatiguing metal.

The next morning April woke with her head tilted distinctly lower than her feet. The rain had stopped, but sometime in the night the corrosive sludge flowing beneath the freestanding cabin had finally softened the metal piers, and the floor listed crazily askew. April felt almost as off-kilter as she had the night before, after she'd finished her young cousins' abandoned tin cups full of Mitch's golden whiskey and peach slivers.

Mitch slept late into the morning. April and her cousins moved about the large room loading backpacks with blankets, with candles, with cans of things they liked to eat. April filled one for Mitch, though the muscles near her heart tightened against her ribs each time she silently rehearsed telling him they were leaving. When he finally woke, she and her three little cousins stood together, booted and fully dressed. April had given the younger ones the remaining rain cloaks and made do with just a heavy wool camping jacket for herself. It itched, and her nose tingled with unspent sneezes.

Mitch stood unsteadily. The Johnson girl had woken earlier, but when April told her they meant to leave and tried to take her hand, she'd shaken her head mutely and closed her eyes and pretended to sleep. She opened them now, but remained on the floor with her face to the ceiling and her arms straight down tight against her sides.

"Mitch, we're leaving. All of us." April held out the backpack she'd loaded for him and pointed to the best pair of boots.

He said nothing. For the first time in a long time he didn't even look angry. April wanted to take this as a good sign, wanted his silence to mean acceptance. But something in the flatness of his eyes made her heart twitch again.

They departed the tilting cabin single file, April leading the way across the yard along the route with the surest footing. The young cousins followed closely behind, sploshing in muck, the smallest holding the tattered deck of cards close to her chest.

Mitch stumbled somewhat unsteadily behind them. He'd dumped all the food April had packed for him into a heap on the floor and refilled his backpack with golden bottles. His steps produced glass-on-glass tinkling, a strange musical accompaniment to the sucking splash under their boots. The Johnson girl followed, wearing no backpack but wrapped in the ragged quilt that had been her sister's favorite. She clung close behind Mitch, a wraith, a pale shadow of a real girl.

April halted at the top of the rise to gaze out over the flooded valley. The church steeple poked out, a stork-white needle stuck upright in the brackish green-grey. The topmost branches of the elm prickled upward from the lake in twiggy quills. But the Johnson's silo was gone, and there was no longer any sign of the shingled roof of the house where April and Mitch had been born.

They descended the ridge to the cliff's edge, lake lapping over the rim after the most recent rains. Heavy clouds receded across the horizon, hazy sky reflecting in sludge sea with a dark oily hue. April squatted and unzipped her pack to rummage for the nearest can. Her cousin Sam offered her a can-opener from his pocket, and she smiled thanks at him. He smiled back, tentative, and she realized with a stab in her side how long it had been since he'd laughed.

She opened the can—stewed tomatoes this time, whole and soft like small detached hearts. She dug out one slippery red glob and held it over the water. "Sea monster whale lake fish, where are you?" she called, her voice rolling away across the grey-green lake in muted echo.

The surface swelled near the cliff edge, and the fish's familiar rounded bulk broke the water in a shower of acidic green fluid. April ignored the prickle and burn on her cheeks where liquid spattered her face. The fish's sides quivered with the sucking of its air-exposed gills, and its jutting unhinged jaw yawned.

The Good Old-Fashioned Kind of Water

April tossed the tomato into its maw, then another, then the whole can all at once. The jaw lowered and the fish's side-fins fanned sludge.

April extended her hand out over the muck and the fish came so close to the edge, lakewater sloshed across the toes of her boots. She stroked the mottled hide, noticing for the first time that it was more scales than skin, though fused together to make a smooth undersurface for acid-etched pitting. Maybe it was just a gargantuan mutant fish like Mitch said, and not something more whalesque or monsterish.

It leaned into her touch like an enormous cold humpbacked cat with no fur. She stroked it, running her hand up its side as it sank low enough in liquid to cover its gills, just eyes and the ridge of its top fin rising above. Holding her breath, April leaned onto the creature's back, inching forward until she lay splayed across it sideways. There was nothing to grasp, no handholds of any kind, but if she moved slowly, she could shimmy toward the animal's head and sit upright. She ignored her stinging skin where moisture from the fish's hide coated her legs. The animal was cold as ice, but the acidic damp burned hot as melted lead.

Gripping tight with her knees, she extended her hand to her nearest cousin. The girl visibly shook, but Sam guided first her, then his other sister to April's outstretched arm. The creature beneath shuddered as each child climbed onto its humped back and scrabbled with small numb fingers at its hide; but April patted it, leaning low over its head to speak soothing nonsensical syllables close to the mottled rubbery surface.

April reached for the Johnson girl but the redhead stepped behind Mitch, her eyes unblinking beneath the cowl of her quilt shroud, wide and dark in a face white as a snow owl's.

April held her hand to Mitch but he wouldn't meet her eyes. He looked at the cliff-edge and the rising mottled bulk of the lake creature and shook his head.

"No goddamn way," he said. He turned to trudge up the mountainside in the direction of the dissolving camping cabin in the skeletal leafless woods.

"Mitch!" April called after his departing back, her voice thin and more watery than the liquid splashing beneath the soles of her dangling boots. "Mitch!"

But he continued climbing the ridge and didn't look back. The cousin gripping April's waist shifted and sucked her breath, and April again felt the burning on her thighs and the insides of her knees where corrosive damp soaked her clothes. She imagined the blisters they'd have when they reached the other side of the valley.

…If we reach the other side of the valley.

She bit her tongue hard and tasted blood, metallic like the water of canned vegetables. *When*, she told herself, gripping the creature's back even tighter as it buoyed higher in the lake and glided forward with its smooth slow motion, air pushing past them heavy and silent. *…When we reach the other side.*

As they neared the tilting steeple—reflected in the oily surface of the lake refracted at an angle so it looked like one long spire broken in half—April twisted, craning her neck around to see over her cousins' heads. Two figures stood silhouetted sharply against the greenish clouds at the top of the cliff, and April imagined she felt their gazes long after she'd turned forward again to squint into thickening acid-misted air. She ignored the blisters rising on her cheeks stung by her tears, thinking tears must be quite like the good old-fashioned kind of water anyway, and hardly corrosive at all.

When not on ten wooded acres near Austin, Texas, **Camille Alexa** lives in Portland, Oregon in an Edwardian house with very crooked windows. Her work appears in *ChiZine*, *Fantasy Magazine*, and *Escape Pod*. Her short fiction collection, PUSH OF THE SKY (Hadley Rille Books, 2009), received a starred review from *Publishers Weekly*. More information and an updated bibliography can be found at http://camillealexa.wordpress.com/.

The Drain

M. Palmer

The young spring grass was wet under her bare feet; it licked at her toes and tickled her soles. Leaves crackled beneath her tiny steps, slimy things squirmed, and a damp patch gave way to her weight like a cold, loose slipper. She paused and felt the earth wanting to keep her, bury her in its dark and muddy bosom. She skipped away, bowing and singing in a whisper, "Not now, my lady" while clutching her doll tighter in the crook of her elbow.

The wind blew across the cornstalks and then up and through her thin nightgown. The darkness surrounding her hinted at movement—the hushed cacophony of things she could not see being, building, hunting, dying. She smelled the oranges of the fruit trees, the cattle dung from the barn half a mile away. When she looked back, Grandmother's house was only a deeper shadow amidst the night, scowling at her; the aluminum wind chimes scolded her from the front porch.

The drain rose out of the ditch at the far front corner of Grandmother's yard just beneath the road. She had not yet seen a car pass along it since her arrival in her Grandmother's sputtering green Buick, suffocating in her two sizes too small black dress, squeezed in the backseat with the bumpy-skinned suitcase and her other boxed up belongings.

She rested her palms on the concrete that reached up to her waist. Loose gravel dusted the rim. A large chunk was missing and she saw the rock monster that had come and taken a bite out of it—a very sloppy eater. She laid Angeline atop the rusted iron grating and peered inside, the half-moon's light leaking down deep into the hole. Clumps of oak leaves and cornstalk debris, mud, and a paper-slim pool of water reflecting back the star-dazzled sky above her. She crinkled her nose at the sweet and sour stench of stagnant water. A frail tail of water flowed on to a darker hole beyond, hidden and mysterious, as black as her sleep or the other side of the moon, as black as she imagined death.

Abby came here in the deep end of night after her Grandmother had fallen asleep (her bear-like snores rattling the floorboards) because…well, because she could. And because if her dreams were real and her prayers were answered, and her mommy leave the ground into which she had been slowly lowered by crank and metallic poles, then Abby knew she would come through that black hole and up and out of this drain. And who else but Abby would be here to help her and greet her with the tightest, warmest hug that ever was given?

Her skin was cold; mud coated her legs. She was seven years old and knew that there was no Santa Claus, that people on TV were actors, that most adults were disappointed and sad, and that the dead did not come back to the living—ever.

But still…She sat down and hugged the concrete in her arms, felt its frozen, rough surface against her cheek like the softest, warmest flesh.

*

Veering across the road, she tried to light her sixth cigarette of the last half hour, one right after the other, never easing the pressure of her bare foot on the gas pedal.

"Screw you!" she cursed, as an old timer in a blue pick-up blared his horn and flailed hairy arms out the window at her.

She jerked the wheel back, exhaling a stream of smoke, and slammed her palm into the soft cushion of the steering wheel. Took another long drag.

She turned up the heavy metal on the radio, music she did not like but felt she needed in this wasteland of corn rows, insectile tractors, and bare, weed-strewn fields. That never-ending, gold-green horizon as empty as a void.

Underneath her sweat, her skin itched. She had panic attacks at the sight of week-old road kill shoved onto unmarked berm. Animal shit honored as incense, rotting grain silos nailed to the horizon.

She coughed and rubbed at her burning eyes. The road curved and wound back in persistent, sometimes sharp, arcs until you felt trapped in a circular maze, getting nowhere, like a pit bull nipping at its own tail. She looked in the rearview mirror as if for an exit, saw her own red, sleep-starved eyes and hollow face, the scabbed lips and dirty, brittle hair and reminded herself for the hundredth time that what the hell…there was nowhere else.

Besides, she came from scarier lands.

The road changed names again, finally into the familiar Lilly Chapel-Kiousville Run. She told herself she recognized the scattered farm houses, the condemned barns, the patterns of forest and field.

Then, so sudden it snatched her breath, there it was—Grandmother's house. Colonial, white with green shutters, sharp gables, taller than it was wide, a wrap around porch its only garnishment. A reef within this sea of cornfields. Withered but still standing like some other-willed junkie.

She slammed on her brakes and spun into the gravel drive, knocking her head against the doorframe. Blood blackened her vision as she skidded to a stop

The Drain

halfway down the drive.

Silence buzzed both inside her head and out.

She picked up a dirty T-shirt from the floor and pressed it against the cut above her eye, adding it to her list of well-won wounds. She cleared off the passenger seat and lay back, lit another cigarette as her hand quivered.

From somewhere a tractor rumbled, sparrows chirped in the oaks above her. The air hung heavy and fetid inside this junked up Volvo bought three days ago with her last couple grams of meth from some slumming New York University student.

She saw the catch basin at the far corner of the front yard as unremarkable as a drain could be on this unremarkable strip of land in this sickeningly unremarkable town amidst this vastly unremarkable, shitty life.

Yet her iron stomach soured and stirred, and she turned on her side and leaned her head over the ash-thickened carpet afraid she would vomit.

She pressed the T-shirt deeper into the cut until it sang and kept her eyes shut.

*

The cool kiss of a sudden burst of wind woke her. Abby yawned and dug her feet deeper into the grass, imagined the hundreds of insects she traumatized in the midst of their secret, busy lives. Angeline smiled at her as always.

Somewhere far away a wild dog howled. The cornstalks trembled. Why did she feel so safe when during the day, in the smells of her Grandmother's potatoes and puddings, she felt so deadly alone?

Below her the water softly echoed. If she carried love seeds in her fists she could crush them into the ground with her heels and teach them how to grow and never trim them until they became as wild and tangled as her own will.

She stood and looked into the drain. Nothing moved. She closed her eyes and furrowed her brow. Waited. Opened them again to see that nothing had stirred. Watched her spit ripple through the scum.

She lit upon an idea. A sudden white glare like when Mommy had come in and flipped on the bedroom lights after a nightmare had chased the screams from her mouth. What Mommy would have called "a moment of complete clarity."

Angeline was long-haired and pale with dark eyes and a warm, close-mouthed smile. Mommy had made her and given her to Abby one day not long before her death when she was too sick to get out of bed. "Look how pretty she is, Abby," she had said in her scarred voice and with wetness in her eyes. Abby knew Mommy said this because she did not think she, herself, was so pretty anymore, and Abby was about to tell how pretty she still was when Mommy smiled and hugged them both, so tightly, and told her Angeline would be hers forever and never leave and how happy that was. "I put a part of me inside her," she had said.

Abby strained and pulled until the iron grating scraped across the concrete just enough. She held Angeline a full arm's length out over the drain. Angeline was filled with stuffing and love, she would be fine. Abby let her go.

Water splattered lightly, the mud hissed.

Mommy would have to come now and return Angeline to keep true what she had promised. And if she didn't, perhaps Mommy needed Angeline more.

Abby waited. Listened to the groans of the oak trees, the rattles of the cornstalks.

Angeline lay face up in muck near the black hole; the shadows of the oaks leaves shuddered over her smile. Abby began to regret what she had done. Angeline had been the last thing Mommy had given her. It was mean, inconsiderate. Mommy might take it the wrong way.

A cloud passed over the moon and all Abby could see in the drain was a rising darkness.

She was about to run to the house and wake Grandmother when she heard something.

She lowered her face into the hole. Pointed her ear down until she heard it again.

A voice. Choked on mud and roots.

"Hello…"

*

"Hello? Abby? Abby Wells?"

The face that peered in at her through the open window was red and puffy; his eyes small and greedy. The man smiled a faceful of square, yellow teeth.

She made him for an asshole immediately.

"You alright?"

She sat up, rubbed her eyes.

"You the lawyer?"

"That's me, Ronald Macklin at your service."

He tipped his cowboy hat and stuck his hand into the car, fingernails stained by some recent meal.

"Most people call me Sparky."

He laughed and stood up, the swell of his belly and sunken crotch thrust at her face. She threw the bloody T-shirt underneath the seat and rummaged for another pack of Marlboros.

He stroked his russet goatee.

"Because of this I suppose…and, well, I'm a bit of a piston."

He cocked an imaginary gun and fired off a volley of chuckles. She stared at him, cigarette dangling from her mouth. Struck the flint with her thumb.

"Well, Ronald. If you'll step back a few feet, I'll get on out."

His chuckled, grunt-like.

The sun stung her eyes. A soft breeze blew her short, stringy hair about her face. The house stood quiet and mediocre and a little unfriendly.

The Drain

"I'm sorry you missed the funeral, but…"

He paused and stared at the bruises and needle tracks on her arms. She moved around him to the backdoor.

"You were a tough one to locate, little lady."

His sudden sour air of superiority and sweaty attraction was as strong as his Brut cologne.

She shrugged.

"Just as well. We didn't know each other much."

She grabbed the duffel bag from the backseat. Felt his eyes on her. They were all the same, city or sticks, animal or educated. Caught a whiff of feminine fragility and they were on the prowl, holding out their grubby, chubby paws with piles of sugar on them assuming no one could say no.

"Here, let me…"

He lunged for the bag. She stuck out her forearm and gave him a shove.

"No, I got it."

He shrugged and grabbed his buckle, hitched up his pants.

"You stayed with her, right?"

"For a short time when I was a girl. After my mother died."

"Well, she left you quite a piece here. Almost five acres. Not enough for farming but plenty to stroll about on."

He held out his arm to take her in as they walked toward the house but she kept ahead just outside his reach. Bottles clanged together in the duffel bag at her side.

"Secluded but town's only ten miles north. Get anything you should need there. The Freemans, that's their corn, live up the road and are real nice folks. The house is agin' but in decent shape. They made things to last out here, had to with the wind. Best of all, it's paid off. She made her social security and the little she got out of your grandfather's accident at the granary go a long way."

He stopped her.

"Look, I don't mean to influence you and I don't know what your plans might be, but I know a lot of people who have their eye on this place and would give up quite a bit for it."

The porch steps groaned under their weight. He lifted up a loose sheet of siding and pulled out a key. The scream door screamed as he swung it open.

"Well, let me show you—"

"I'm fine here, Macklin."

He looked at her, mouth open and waiting for a treat. She took the key from his hand.

"Well, okay. But there's some things about the house you should know. You won't need it but there is a security system. The code is 0119—shouldn't be hard for you to remember." He winked at her.

It made her squirm. He probably knew everything about her. That was one thing the city and all the clustered, rat-trapped places she'd been had going for them over a place like this. There, you were always an unknown, part of an ever-mutable scenery; here, everyone knew you as intimately as the local mortician would at your death.

"The shingles need replaced. No washer or dryer. No dishwasher either. Mmmmmm. You understand about the bad stair that caused your Grandmother…well, it ain't fixed, but I took the liberty of calling Jimmy Dulcet. He'll be in maybe after the weekend."

She squinted at him and nodded as she stood in between the front door and the screen.

"Listen," he said, and stepped closer to her. "I know you've had some hard times and don't know anybody around here."

"I've been a stranger everywhere I've lived."

"So you realize how nice it is to have a friend. Let me take you into town, get us fed, introduce you to some nice people, show you a good time."

"Nope."

She stared at him. He hovered, breathed deep.

"Okay, then, Abby Wells. I'll leave you to it."

He started down the steps as she turned and unlocked the door, stepped inside to the stale air.

"Maybe I'll come back later on tonight and check on you. I could bring a fine bottle of spirits. Let me do something nice for you."

He looked up at her, smiling full. A real thick, stubborn one like all the redheads she had encountered. Especially the older, well-fed, male ones.

"Not if this was my last night on earth, Sparky." She flashed him her widest smile-sneer.

He laughed and whistled and tugged on his belt and continued on down the path. As his boots scuffed over the gravel his whistle continued, the first shrieked note calming into a chirpy melody.

*

Like the soft clackings of rodent feet, the voice echoed up the cold walls of the drain before fading in the air around Abby's face, swept off by the wind.

"Hello, Princess."

Stronger but still frail. Abby did not know if it was man or woman, adult or child. She dared not answer.

"I know you're up there. I can see you. So pretty in the moonlight."

Abby ducked down beneath the concrete, covered her mouth.

"Don't be afraid. Come back, sweetie. I can't hurt you."

She looked back to the shadow-enveloped house, so far away. The cornstalks breathed their dry breath.

"Please, don't leave me alone."

Abby slowly rose and peeked one eye over the edge. She thought she heard it sigh. A smell curled up into her nose—stale corn or her mother's bed. Abby's bellybutton had been infected once. It stunk like this in short, pungent bursts.

"Don't you love the night? The feeling of being the only one awake amidst all this sleeping stuff? You know, if you close your eyes and listen you can hear all of their dreams."

Abby closed her eyes. The thing in the drain hacked—flutter of dead leaves.

"Have you ever thought a dream real? More real than being awake? Have you ever wanted it to be so?"

It moved. A misshapen shudder in the darkness. The wet plop of mud; a scratch against the rock.

"Is this yours?"

Angeline's face turned up into the moon's full light, and with it, fingers as earthen and bony as winter tree limbs.

"Don't you want her back?"

*

The face that met her in the living room mirror across from the front door was pale and sallow. The eyes heavy-lidded and colorless, blood smeared in their whites. Wrinkles like dried up riverbeds spread out from the corners of her eyes, dark sunken bruises like rotten fruit beneath. Skin thin and ungiving, lips dry and cracked. There were scars and ruptured capillaries. She was twenty-seven and twin to a corpse.

At age thirteen, after five years spent in and out of hospitals, she escaped from the psychiatric center and ran, hid, and hitchiked her way three hundred miles south to St. Louis. But she had never truly settled. Like a foot-bound shark, death if she ever stopped her manic movement. From curb to curb, city to city. Always in the heart of a metropolis with its chaotic conglomerates of brick and steel, traffic and smog, and most importantly, its thick, endless herd of others she could live amongst without memory.

For a long time she lived in the streets. She learned to sift through the scraps of trash bins and outdoor tables, to stay warm huddled in her own arms through frozen air and ice-slick streets. She slept on the loose gravel and blacktops of alleyways, grand church steps, the concrete slabs slanting down into foul rivers. She lay with rodents and dirty old men, within the piles of noisy, smelly strangers in sepulcher-like subways. She learned to be one of them, one of the countless many like a pebble in the pavement.

She learned the basic, stoic, human transaction of free trade—one favor for another. She sold whatever she had or could get; she offered blowjobs and gold-plated bracelets behind overflowing dumpsters. She learned to eat like a snake, drink like a camel. She knew the sounds of gunfire and sirens hot in her ears, of curses and screams, of shattered glass and the soft, meaty thuds of fists against flesh. Tastes in her mouth that could never be brushed away. She knew the constant, thus deadened, buzz-dread of being surrounded by violent men. She learned to cut herself often; it helped.

She knew of poverty; poverty in words, in feelings, of dreams. The jackhammer of hours surviving. She knew the claustrophobia of a jail cell and the empty expanse of men she loathed fondling and stabbing deep inside her. She learned how it was to be a rat: sniffing, searching with every clawed step; no corner unexamined, no hole condemned, until finding not food but a baggie of dust. She knew of marriage followed with divorce, and birth (the squirming, determined head splitting her open) followed by the sight of her son, small and stiff and blue in his crib. She knew reasonlessness and chaos, her overwhelmingly small insignificance within the crammed sea of indifference.

She knew of death, had known it as everyone did from the moment the umbilical cord was cut from around her throat. But she had come to learn of a life that was far worse than death.

*

"Who are you?"

Half her nose peeked over the concrete. She spoke softly and in spurts like rabbit hops.

"Just a voice."

She lifted her face a little more.

"What are you doing down there?"

There was movement—a rustling, slithering. A cough full of pinecones and leaves and dandelion seeds.

"I'm hiding or I'm trapped. I can't remember which. Maybe I'm crazy. I'm thinking of a curse. A once happy life undone by a horrific happenstance. Such things befall us sometimes. Perhaps I did something very bad. Maybe I've just been forgotten."

"Isn't it icky down there?"

"Oh, it's not bad. You get used to it. Can be quite enjoyable if you don't mind the bugs and the smells and the loneliness. *And* if you know what to watch and listen for. Sometimes special things find their way down here."

"Like Angeline?"

"Just like Angeline. All sorts of special things. Pretty balls, strange creatures, sad poems. Coins and rings and old toys. Love letters and photographs and thumb-stained books. Drawings and wishes. Echoes and memories. Prayers. Just the other day I found this bent key. What could it open? And will it ever be opened again?"

Abby jumped up and leaned out over the drain.

"Do you collect them?"

"Oh, yes. I collect them all. I love them. You could say I feed on them in a way. They keep me alive."

*

114

The Drain

Abby set the duffel bag on the round, sauce-stained oak table in the kitchen. In twenty years the house had not changed; it was smaller, less imposing, but that was due to changes in Abby and not in any evolutions in her Grandmother's tastes. Same Rockwell and agricultural paintings on the walls, same white lace curtains, same hardwood floors and wheat-patterned wallpaper. The soft, pendulum sway of the wall clock was like the beat of her heart—rote, insignificant.

In the sink there was a plate dotted with cake crumbs and a coffee mug with a thick, black ring crusting at the bottom. Abby scrubbed and dried them and put them away. A half-eaten apple, all brown on the inside, sat on the counter. A fly flew up from it when she threw it away. The refrigerator was forlorn with tubs of butter and creamer, a few cheese singles, soured milk, a head of leaking lettuce, a couple of eggs and a yogurt. The freezer was full with popsicles and indistinguishable, freezer-burnt meat. No matter. Her appetite, if any, groaned for a different sort of satisfaction.

She pulled the bottles from the bag one by one and stacked them on the table. Jack Daniels, Jose Cuervo, Absolut, Jagermeister, and a Glenlivet 20, a last luxury. Couple cans of cola and Red Bull.

She poured a glass of the Glenlivet. Smooth. That was what money got you—made it easier to swallow shit. She lit a cigarette, breathed, kept drinking. The sun fell below the corn, cut a swath through the stalks and bled scarlet across the table. A thousand still and silent witnesses as faceless as any crowd.

Cigarette ash collected in little mounds on the floor. She held the thin sliver of razor in the last of the blood-red light. She did not know how to feel since, of course, she felt nothing at all.

*

"Do you want her back?"
Abby nodded.
"I know you do. But you'll have to help me."
"How?"
Abby thought of promises, of vials of blood and her soul or her first born son. Of obtaining a lock of witch's hair or some long lost, powerful stone. Of taking its place down there in the cold, wet darkness.
"You'll have to let me out."
Abby sighed and turned her back to the drain, sat down on the lip.
"What is it, Princess?"
"I don't think I can."
"Of course you can."
"I don't know. I don't know if I should. I'm scared."
The thing in the drained moved. Abby could feel its eyes on her back.
"Look there above you. Do you know what that is?"
A light singed the blue-black sky for a brief, shuddering moment, a tail of

sparks trailing behind, and then disappeared.

"A shooting star," she answered. Abby made a wish but did not speak it.

"Yes, and do you know what a shooting star is?"

"A falling star."

"Yes! Exactly! Falling. Falling from its high seat in the heavens. Falling because it is dying."

Clouds covered the moon. The world made no sound.

"Think of it. All that glorious, life-giving light so old and massive and brilliant—even it too must perish. The most grand, powerful, beautiful thing can't escape. At that very moment, as we watched, it died and all that life it created and sustained died too. A thousand worlds a thousand times larger than this one you and I are on. And there it has happened again! Look! Another! Don't you feel how sad it is?"

The sky was awash in falling stars, bursts of shuddering light slicing open the night, falling into each other, into blackness.

"But it's beautiful too, isn't it? What does the dying star do in its final moment? It gives a moment of unequaled brilliance. A brilliant, breath-taking glory of fire that whoever sees it can never forget."

Abby could not take her eyes away from them. It was awesome. She felt good, safe. Like her body was more than able to hold her all in. Like being in her mother's arms.

"Someday, somebody will tell you different. They will bring books and photographs and tell you a shooting star is not a dying one. That it is not falling. That it is not even a star. But remember what I've told you. It's truer than whatever they'll say."

Abby turned and looked down into the drain.

"Okay. I'll do it. I'll help you out."

*

She turned on the light and shielded her eyes from the brightness. Took a drink of Jack and gripped the bottle tight in her fist.

The bedroom was as she had left it. Dusted and swept consistently over the years but the contents untouched. Ponies on the nightstand, a pink quilt with her name and birth date nailed to the wall above the bed, a bookshelf full of picture books and fairy tales. Stuffed animals littered the bed, all furry limbs and stitched smiles. Thumb-tacked to the wall were drawings of little girl hopes and little girl fears: colorful forests and unicorns flying past the sun; sharp-clawed, teeth-baring beasts full of smoke and anger and unnamable intent.

She felt nauseous, unbalanced. Had twenty years happened? But of course they had. God, she had lived them—she had the scars to prove it. Unreal were the years before she had escaped, in the moments she now looked at as she flipped through the photograph book her mother had made in a last desperate effort for immortality. She had no feelings for the bright-eyed, chubby-cheeked girl in the photographs. She could not remember these framed moments, the facts behind them or the emotions within. The only thing she felt looking at the pictures was how weird that the girl in them had ceased to exist, her reality as brief and burning as a candle flame, or if she did in a sense survive it was in a world and time from which she could never escape, that never ended or evolved, for there was no cord or sentiment connecting her to the present adult incarnation.

There was only one moment she could not forget no matter how far she ran or how numbed her mind. Abby turned off the light and went to the window. She could see it in the darkness—the cylindrical blackness rising from the weeds.

It was lifetimes ago, lifetimes, but this could be the morning after the way that night now seemed so omnipotent, omnipresent. She had become someone else, but here everything stood waiting and unchanged as if nothing had happened in the time between. She felt the cold stirrings of that old terror, the night that could not have been, that made no sense, but had certainly set her path. She had never thought of it until now, but here it was as clear as taking a cloth to a dirty mirror and cleaning its stains and water marks and casually surrendered bodily fluids. That night had brought her here to this moment.

She chuckled, took another swig, sucked her cigarette to the filter. Such realizations did not matter one fucking cent.

Her life was what it had been. It had happened. The past was not alive, nor were nightmares, and certainly not dreams. The only real thing was now.

She opened her hand to the razor blade resting in her palm. There was nothing so real as this. The simple straight edge, sharp and cold. Perfectly formed to its function.

She had not even noticed the cut it had already made, the thin line of blood in her hand, bright and vulnerable as a child's mind.

*

"Good girl."
Down in the darkness a flash of light like the ivory of eyes or of teeth.
"Now, wait for me."

*

It was a short walk, not the journey she remembered.

The night was full, the road empty. The grass was dry and brittle against her feet, the earth hard and uneven. The last swallow of whisky sloshed around at the bottom of the bottle. She felt hollow as the wind licked at her skin, whistled in her ears.

The drain reached only to the middle of her thighs. Dead leaves scattered, the drip-drop of dirty water. Innocuous as a forgotten lie.

She put the bottle to her lips, staggered back on her heels. The alcohol trickled easily down her throat.

Of course what she remembered had not happened. All the doctors in all the white, windowless rooms had made that clear. Hallucination. Post-traumatic Stress Disorder. Adolescent Dementia. The Nightmarish Fancies Of An Overly Anxious, Sad Little Girl.

And they were right. Such things did not, could not happen. There were worse things, real things. Plenty had happened to her.

She lifted the grating and slid it with ease. Held the bottle out over it. She followed the moonlight down into the muck and saw, half buried in leaves and corn husks, two black eyes and a pale, plastic cheek.

And then a moist rustling like crows at war in the cornfields.

*

She did not know how it climbed the smooth, cylindrical walls, but she watched the shadow slowly rise and heard it too: the scraping against rock followed by a spongy slithering, the tumble of gravel beneath its steady progress. Her face held up into the moonlight, Angeline inched forward out of the darkness above the amorphous shadow.

"Abby..."

*

"Mommy."

Like the wind through the corn. She fell to the ground her back against the drain. The bottle tumbled from her hand.

Of course there was nothing there. She was alone. The smell of oranges going bad in the scrub grass.

Silence. White fingertips pressing the edge of the razor into her palm. Nothing else was real.

She brought the razor down to the soft flesh of her wrist.

"Wait...I'm coming."

The leaves fluttered. Reflected in the bottle, she watched the tiny hands emerge into the air above the drain, a curl of fine, blonde hair.

*

She stood above the grating, hands wrapped around the rusty metal. She trembled as the wind peeped under her nightgown. The moon was gone. Blackness filled the drain.

And then something cold, rough brushed her fingertips.

She let go, stumbled back.

A hand appeared from below, curled around the grating. A cloud of dirt and dust and flakes of rotten flesh puffed out into the silver air. The fingers were thin and black and gore-ridden.

"I'm here."

The voice was familiar even choked as it was with gravel and mud. It drew her forward. Abby leaned over the drain.

Mommy's face stared up at her, striped by the grating's shadows. One-eyed, worm-eaten. Lice and maggots and plumper things crawled through her hair.

"Let me out, honey."

*

The little river of blood ran down past her elbow. She exhaled. Surprised to feel the tears.

Her eyes closed, she heard the grating clang to the ground beside her. Something wet and heavy slithered across the concrete and stood. The corn and the oak leaves stilled.

She got to her feet, turned, and opened her eyes.

Saw not her son nor her mother, but herself standing naked before her. Skeletal limbs bloodless and blue, breasts like deflated balloons, eyes black and wet. The thing that was her held its arms out toward her, the twin gashes that ran the length of its forearms quivering, gulping for air. Under the pale blue moon it walked forward.

This was what death was. This was dying.

She came and wrapped herself in an embrace.

*

Everything went black. She fell to the earth; her screams had no sound. Her mother's voice calling, begging; her skinless hands held the grating, beating against it, struggling to open it.

Abby ran and ran and ran.

*

Everything was light.

Her touch was cold like the breath of the dead, like the rivers underneath the earth, like moonlight. But as she held herself there was the heat of blood, the warmth of dawn sprinkling over dew-tipped fields, of thawing.

She remembered lilacs—how her mother pressed them into books—and the smooth perfection of laminate. She remembered tea and old fancy clothes and the happiness in her mother's laughing green eyes. She remembered graham cracker pudding, baths, kickballs, flashlights dancing in the dark. The smell of her mother's silk nightgowns and the sound of popcorn popping in the microwave. She remembered the taste of cold pasta, the scent of leather, the feel of oil on her skin. The freedom of a city street at night, its earnest hope at dawn. Cinnamon-scented soap, pillows, coffee, a key unlocking a door. The satisfaction of cashing a check, the sweet spark of meeting a stranger's eye. The absolution of tears and the angry tender submission ingestion exhaustion of sex. The way a train sounded from a midnight's distance. Bra-less days and rotating fans and to say the words "I love you." Listening to her baby's nonsense babble in his crib, the dance of pacifiers in his hands. His still, contented clinging. Rubbing noses, fingering his fine hair, basking in his uncontaminated smile. Taking turns pressing buttons on a colored keyboard. The playful weight that remained inside her no matter how far away he went.

That and so much more stripped clean.

She felt each one succinctly and everything all at once like a bomb, like a slow immersion into white bright light.

There was a flash and then it was gone leaving flaming, falling remnants behind. Inside of her and all across the distant sky.

*

The red Cadillac rolled into the gravel drive and disappeared into the dirt clouds that puffed up around it. Abby sat on the porch steps in jean shorts and a tank top, cradling a coffee mug in her hands. Jimmy Dulcet's hammerings inside the house punctuated the rumbling from the granary up the road. She took a sip then grinned as Ronald Macklin strode up the stone path. She squinted up at him.

"Mr. Macklin."

"Sparky, remember?"

He chuckled and stooped down to shake her hand. Smacked his spearmint gum.

"I was happy to hear your message. Sensible decision. Lots of people with their eye on this place. Easy sale."

"First I'm going to work on this place some. Clean it up. Get some new flooring, paint, maybe some a/c and appliances. I have some decorating ideas."

"Well, let me get some people out here."

"I can handle it, Sparky. Just give me some time. No rush is there?"

"Nope. Not at all. That's one thing about us out here; we take our time getting to where we're going."

His eyes stopped at the bandages on her arms, then lingered over her legs.

"I'll tell you, Miss Wells, you make quite a bit better sight than you did the other day. I was worried about you."

"I feel good, Sparky."

"Hey, that sure is pretty."

He pointed to the doll lying beside her. Abby picked it up, wiped away a bit of dirt from its eye.

"You got any little daughters? Nieces? A grandbaby or two?"

The Drain

He laughed.

"Maybe one or two."

"Take it."

She held Angeline up to him. Ronald Macklin took it into his thick hands, gently.

"Well, that's mighty kind—"

He went on but her eyes were already drawn back to the horizon and the palettes of blue there and somewhere within, certain but invisible, the myriad of stars.

M. Palmer resides in West Jefferson, Ohio with his wife and two children. He is a graduate of the Miami (Ohio) creative writing program. His work has appeared in such fabulous venues as *Fantasy Magazine* and the anthology *Tattered Souls* from Cutting Block Press. He can be reached at palmer.239@osu.edu.

M. Palmer would like to express his indebtedness to PJ Harvey and her album *White Chalk* during the creation of this story.

Cold

Melissa S. Green

"What does cold feel like?" Lys asked.

It wasn't Masozi who'd been asked, but it was Masozi who answered. "If you want to know that," he said, "you go stand under the shower and turn off all the hot. It makes your skin stand up in bumps."

Everyone stared at him, eyes wide with the unconsidered adventure of it.

"What?" he demanded. "You've never tried it?" Bai had, but she wasn't going to say so. "None of you? If you stand under the shower long enough, it gives you a bad headache."

"Must've had a big stiffie, to stay under that long, Masozi," Gavril said. "Ana turn you down for a date, yeah?"

Everyone laughed. Even Boleyn laughed, who didn't know Masozi, his family having come down planetside only a year ago. For a moment Bai could imagine they were really here just to share tea and a few laughs to welcome Boleyn back. But she knew Lys. All her life she knew Lys. Boleyn was wrong if she thought that was the end of the question.

"So is that what it's like, Boleyn?" Lys demanded when the laughter died down. "Is it like Masozi said?"

"It can be," Boleyn admitted slowly. "But most often, you're clothed and dry, and still it's cold."

It would've been better had she simply said yes, Bai thought.

"Well, but what if you had on all your clothes and went into the meat freezer right here at Commons?" Walker asked. He aimed his thumb behind him, toward the walk-ins. "That would be like the Cold, yeah?"

Lys nodded. "Yeah, yeah, that would be." She looked at Boleyn. "Wouldn't it, then?"

Of course not, Bai thought, *how stupid. But just say yes. She's baiting you, can't you see?*

Boleyn said, "Somewhat."

Cold

"Somewhat?" Lys said. "Somewhat? What's different, then?"

Boleyn's face had become very still. Wary, it seemed to Bai. Good. Hadn't she described what Lys was like now, at least once? Be wary. Boleyn said, "There's nothing in there you can burn."

"Huh?" Walker grunted. "What's that count?"

They really didn't know much about cold, did they? Hadn't any of them even talked with someone on coldcrew?

"You can't make a fire with frozen meat," Boleyn explained. "So you'd become frozen meat yourself."

"Frozen meat," Gavril repeated with a coarse chuckle.

"Well, of course," Lys said scornfully, "that's why they don't put a lock on the meat freezer, so no one gets caught in there. You walk out before you freeze."

Bai laughed. She didn't laugh loudly, but it was enough that Lys turned her way, eyebrow raised in question and reproach. Except for Masozi, they'd all known each other from childhood, and it took no thought for Bai to understand that Lys was perfectly capable of directing her scorn next at her. Fleetingly Bai wondered why she'd ever cared. She found now that she did still care, but not much. Mostly only to consider the folly of having bent to the wind all this time.

Bent to the wind — that was an expression. She'd never actually felt a wind. Now Boleyn was back, who *had* felt the wind. That changed things.

"Well, that's her point, isn't it?" she told Lys. "If you went in the meat locker, you could walk right back out here into Commons the moment you got uncomfortable. But out there, you need the means to make your own comfort. Or else you die. Yeah?"

"Yeah, sure," leered Gavril, whose mind always went to the lewd side of things, "make your own comfort." His arm was moving, no doubt to propel an obscene gesture just under the table.

Now, if she'd wanted to please Lys, Bai should have phrased her observation in one of the many mocking ways — but directed at Boleyn — that had been implicit from Lys' very first question. *What does cold feel like?* from Lys meant, *What is the Cold like?* — meant, *What is it like to be Exiled*, and *Do you think you're really welcome back?* Not that Boleyn had herself been assigned to Test Forest 3, but her parents had, and she'd gone with them, she and her brothers. Now they were back: her parents had done what they were supposed to do, made amends to the community for their crime, stuck out their hard duty in a hard, cold place, and were officially returned to respectability, if not quite popular favor.

But that was Court and Consensus among the generations of their parents and grandparents. They were the next generation, with their own politics. They all had yet to Examine into the full Consensus, with its adult politics and Constitutional ways of assigning authority. *What does cold feel like?* from Lys meant, *You're not welcome here, not until I say so*, meant, *Not until I've humiliated you and you've acknowledged me as leader.* But by way of the

123

respect Bai had offered for whatever skills had carried Boleyn and her family through their years in the Cold, Bai had offered premature welcome. She'd crossed a line. Lys, who thought consensus was built out of manipulation and bullying, would not soon forgive her.

Which also meant she was in trouble with the lot of them. Bai had only to look at Boleyn across the table from her to remind herself that she'd stuck her neck out for someone everyone else regarded as a stranger and an outsider. Boleyn was even dressed differently. All the rest of the youngers, or for that matter everyone else in Commons this morning, were in standard greens; but there Boleyn sat in orange insulated cuvs with the lower sleeves zipped off, like some coldcrew member fresh out of the Empty.

But so what? What else would Bai ever have done? Boleyn was no stranger to her. Hadn't Bai cried, when they'd been all of twelve years old and the Exile of the Maheshwaris had taken Boleyn away with the rest of her family? All the stories they'd ever heard about the Cold told her there was every possibility they'd never see one another again. Five years. In all that time, all they'd had of each other was their letters, written on the rough paper turned out by the Experimental Manufactory. In all that time, she'd never even heard Boleyn's voice: the coldcrews hadn't strung wire that far yet, and the wireless transmitter at Test Forest 3 was on restricted use.

Well, Bai was just as informed as everyone else in Turnbull of Consensus reasoning, affirmed and formalized by Court. The sanction pronounced upon Akash and Elizabeth Maheshwari was just by anyone's estimation, even the Maheshwaris themselves. But it was no fairness to their children, innocent, who to evade Exile would be cut away from their parents, but to join it would be cut from their friends and community.

But they went.

Bai hadn't even known what Boleyn looked like anymore, not after five years. One changed a lot in the years from age twelve to age seventeen. Taller now by a few inches, Boleyn was, and not so skinny anymore – she now had a good solid leanness to her. And her hair was... shorter?... yes. Still that shiny black, but it extended now only to her nape, whereas she used to wear it down her shoulders. Her face's shape had changed, too: like the rest of her body. Lean, not skinny and sharp as before. Her eyes were still brown, but there was now a reserve to them, an unease, where Bai remembered them as being lit up with laughter and mischief. Or maybe it was just the circumstance she was in now, a returned exile being prodded at by those who had never been cast away.

Wonder how I've changed to her, Bai thought. They'd been best friends. Then...nothing except what they could fit in letters two or three times a year. Somehow they still knew each other so well, or at least that's what she had wanted to believe. But they'd been shy and awkward since first meeting again this morning. And their awkwardness hadn't had time to rub off before Lys and everyone had barged in to their Kitchen to interrupt. What if it never rubbed off?

Lys stretched theatrically and got up. Offended, no doubt, but having learned that it wasn't dignified to go off in a temper. "C'mon," she said languidly, and Gavril and Walker obediently got up, taking their mugs with them. Masozi was slower to rise, and then he lingered. "I'm Masozi," he introduced himself, offering his hand to Boleyn. "We just came down from Station a few months ago. But... well... welcome back. Good to meet you."

"Thanks," Boleyn said, taking his hand. "Well met."

Well, that was one take on it. But no, Masozi was all right. He wasn't lockstep with everything Lys wanted. He was more like Bai, just *bending with the wind*, but going his own way when he wanted. Beyond him, Lys betrayed an impatient scowl at his back and stalked off. By the time Masozi turned to follow, she, Gavril, and Walker had disappeared from Commons towards Library tube. Masozi threw a grin at Bai, shrugging, and went another direction.

Then it was just Bai with Boleyn again in their little corner of Green Commons, and again the awkward, shy silence.

"I didn't remember Lys was like that," Boleyn ventured.

"Oh. Well. I think she was. Didn't I write you about her? She wants us back in the days of kings and queens and presidents, with her as World Emperor. Ma thinks she's got a big shock coming to her when we join adult Consensus, and turns out she'll be just another younger like us."

"Oh." Boleyn stared down at her mug, swirling her tea around in it. "Isn't she already just another younger like us?"

That made Bai laugh, and Boleyn look up at her. "She is at that. I'm not real sure how we got to letting her lord it over us."

Boleyn smiled, then. It wasn't an easy relaxed smile, but in it Bai began to see a hint of the girl she'd known five years ago, when they were seldom out of each other's company. "I guess she won't like me very well, then. Not much good at being lorded over. *It's not the Consensus way*," she quoted in a ironic tone. She put her mug down. "It's so strange to be back here. It's... very strange. So many people..."

So many people. So many she'd missed, when she'd first left. Boleyn's earliest letters had been suffused with loneliness. All she'd had at Test Forest 3 were her brothers and parents and the few who lived and worked there by way of normal assignment: none of her friends. By comparison, Bai's life hadn't changed much at all: same Kitchen, same Commons, same family and peer group and friends.

Except that Boleyn was far away, and she was the friend who counted most. And so Bai had been full of loneliness too. The only times the loneliness went away was when a letter from Boleyn arrived, written in that painstaking cursive they'd both taught themselves out of Library when they were ten, like a code so no one else could read it. When a letter came, something would take the place of the loneliness inside her, some kind of peculiar joy, forming up inside her like a bubble or a balloon, growing larger and larger until it exploded out of her in a vast and almost hysterical happiness. It was a crazy enough feeling that she instinctively hid it from everyone, pulling it instead close to herself, husbanding and nourishing it in privacy to try to make it last as long as possible.

It worked, somewhat. But the loneliness always sifted in again, until she grew accustomed to it, a little hollow inside herself as she went through her days.

Boleyn must have done much the same. After the first year, her letters stopped speaking of loneliness or missing people. They filled up instead with accounts of the things she was experiencing and learning, written out in slow, thoughtful, deeply considered sentences that made Bai feel, in reading them, as if she was seeing into Boleyn's very mind and heart, more so even than when they were children running wild and mischievous through the length and breadth of Turnbull's habitats, sleeping over at each other's places almost as often as at their own, talking and giggling until they fell asleep.

Now, some two hundred kilometers away, Boleyn tried to describe, so that Bai could see it, what the remote station was like, and the people in it. *Metsi*, they called the test station, which meant *woods* in some old Earth language someone had dug up in Library. Boleyn would describe, so that Bai could almost feel it, what it was like to go outside in winter. At Turnbull, kids and youngers only ever went out during the brief summers, and only on infrequent, closely-supervised field trips. But Boleyn and her brothers routinely went out even without olders, even in the deepest winter, bundled up in under-layers with coldcuvs and boots and breather. Even then, Boleyn wrote, she'd feel the cold seep in through the outer and inner layers of her clothes to chill her skin, and then burrow under her skin to make her fingers stiff and her toes and cheeks numb. She wrote about what the great Empty was like when she went with her parents or Pina Chomko or Alberto Talvi or other olders out into the sparseness of the decades-old tundra or into the mix of shrubs and scrubby trees that passed for a forest on this briefly inhabited planet, and told Bai about what they taught her: that the Empty was not so empty. That the Cold was warming with life.

And words — words that hadn't been spoken for generations, not since their ancestors left the Planets to settle the Belt and the Six Moons. Words that hadn't been spoken on the ships that came through the Long Dark from Sol System, nor on the stations as the Project slowly progressed to engineer this world, nor even in the permanent habitats that had been now a full two decades on the planet's surface. They were words that appeared only in Library databases, in old books and movies that had come with them all the many years from Earth, describing phenomena that no one of the Project in centuries had any direct experience of. But some of these words were now in Boleyn's parlance: *frostbite, pingo, frost heave, sundog, fog*. She might have looked some of them up, but most she'd been told by olders at Metsi, the first to be reborn to the experiences that gave those words meaning. *Three-hundred year words*, Bai called them: Boleyn taught them to her in her letters, and Bai would look them up to understand them even better, in order to know what Boleyn was experiencing and feeling and thinking.

She did her very best to give back to Boleyn in kind. But she had so few new words to teach her. She was living the same life Boleyn had already known at Turnbull, different only in that Bai was getting older in it, with the maturing perspective of a fourteen and fifteen and sixteen-year-old. It seemed so dull in comparison to what Boleyn was living. Somehow, though, it became more interesting by the very act of writing it out for Boleyn, because Bai wanted to give back to Boleyn what Boleyn was giving to her. She wanted Boleyn to know her mind and heart, too.

It eased her loneliness, she found: her days took on a fascination as she evaluated them for what was worth telling her friend. She'd script out the things she thought to tell about in her System account and then pick out the best bits, the most interesting, and copied them out in careful longhand on the pages of brown Manufactory paper, and collect the pages she wrote over weeks and sometimes months until the next time a coldcrew was sent out on a supply run to the test station. Her pages would go out, and Boleyn's would come back.

So she knew something of what cold felt like, and what life was like for the few humans who lived in it. She supplemented what Boleyn taught her by talking with Nikos, her coldcrew friend, and by reading the reports filed on-System by Pina Chomko and Alberto Talvi and monitoring their conversations on the eco-wiki. So she knew more than most youngers about what they did and the signs they saw that the Project was succeeding. In her own lifetime, they said, they'd be able to walk outside without breathers, something no one had done since Esti Gusev departed Earth to join the Project so many lifetimes ago.

Boleyn, in turn, knew something of what life was at Turnbull, and how it grew and changed in her absence, larger by three Commons and now one not of six but of eight permanent base settlements on the planetary surface. But Turnbull was still strange to her now, perhaps even as strange as the Cold would be to Bai when she went out into it.

It was with that thought that Bai greeted a dream that must've lain hidden in her for months, perhaps even years. She wanted to go out into the Cold. She wanted to see Metsi. And she wanted to do it with Boleyn.

"It's so much bigger, too," Boleyn was saying. "Of course, you told me it was, in your letters... but..." She trailed off, stared down into her mug. "Need more tea," she muttered. She pushed her mug away and looked up. "Bai... I never thought I would, but I got to liking it there, at Metsi. Then one day I realized...the only thing I missed about Turnbull anymore was you." She looked away, hesitant. "And now I'm back... well... I think..." She looked back at Bai. "I want talking to you, face to face, to be like our letters. I don't want it to be like... I don't know. Like that crap with Lys."

Had she thought Boleyn looked different from when they were twelve-year-olds? Taller, more filled-out but still lean, shorter hair... but not, really, that much different. Not with that in her eyes. Not in how the bubble grew inside of Bai and grew until it burst out into that expanse of joy that she had always hugged to herself, private and close.

Time to let it free, just a little. "So we won't be like that crap with Lys," Bai said. "It's not even possible for us to be like that." She reached her hand across the table, taking Boleyn's. "Yeah?"

Melissa S. Green describes herself as 'a workaday workadyke of the north' – working by day as a publication specialist, by night (and lunchtimes) as a writer, poet, and blogger. After spending much of 2009 focusing on local political battles, Mel is now endeavoring to make good on the term 'occasional political blogger' by returning the main focus of her website, and her life, to writing science fiction, fantasy, and poetry. She can be found at Henkimaa.com.

"Cold" is the first chapter of a novel-in-progress.